A Historic Fairway Adventure

Duane's Tee Time Tales

Jesse Satterfield

A Historic Fairway Adventure

Duane's Tee Time Tales

DUANE WILLIAMS

MONICA GUILLEMIN WILLIAMS
Author Black Deception & Cloning

Duane's Tee Time Tales
A Historic Fairway Adventure
Print Edition 1

Vision Harmony

4195 Chino Hills Parkway, Ste. 478
Chino Hills, California 91709
951-505-2503

visionharmony.net
visionharmonyllc.com
facebook.com/vision_harmony
instagram@vision_harmony
visionharmonyllc@gmail.com

ISBN: 978-0-9748715-5-4
LCCN: 2024922877

Printed in USA

A LEGACY ON THE FAIRWAY PRESERVED

Honoring Jesse and Reginald Satterfield

Writing to you here brings a big smile to my face. I see you whenever there's a beautiful sunrise and a window silhouette because I know you're probably up drinking your morning coffee. Duane and I finally finished the book about Grandpa Jesse's golf legacy. I only wish we could have completed it while you were still here, just to witness your proud grin and hear your "Ok, wait, now ho… I told you so." However, there are two other quotes that have always carried me forward: 1). *The early bird gets the worm,* and 2). *Strike while the iron is hot.* Consequentially, Duane and I moved forward with this book.

After you left us, I spent much of the year determined to find that original news article our family had kept all these years in the photo albums. With the help of a kind librarian in Texas' genealogy department and cousin Rita, not only did I find it, but I uncovered so much more about Grandpa Jesse. His story is even richer than we imagined.

Daddy, I discovered Grandpa Jesse wasn't just playing golf—he was one of the first two African American men to play at the historic Brackenridge Golf Course! Can you believe it? Brackenridge—the oldest 18-hole public golf course in the state of Texas and apparently the "first inductee into the Texas Golf Hall of Fame!" It turns out Grandpa Jesse also worked at Oak Hills Country Club, though listed as a 'club house boy' or sometimes a 'house attendant.' He also worked at Willow Springs Golf Course, according to his military registration card naming "Mr. George Hoffman, Willow Springs Golf Course" in San Antonio as his employer when he was just 24 years old. There were even misspellings of his name in nearly every news article including on his death certificate, where he was listed as "Jessie," but Grandpa signed his name proudly as Jesse Satterfield. I made sure to fix that on your own death certificate and also ensured your middle name was spelled correctly so we wouldn't repeat history a generation later.

Since learning Grandpa Jesse's place in history, I've made it my mission to honor his legacy. I'm planning to file petitions to have Brackenridge's 100th-anniversary celebration corrected to include Grandpa Jesse and his friend, Sergeant Edward Green, who made history right alongside him that day. I'll also send this information to the Texas Golf Hall of Fame and the National Museum of African American History & Culture at the Smithsonian, so our family's story—and our people's history—is remembered and honored accurately, without omitting relevant facts.

At some point, I'll go ahead and write the story about Penny Parson, the Penny Parson Estate et al., and the Nickson family legacy she and her daughter Lonnie Nickson left behind. I'm not sure if I'll keep the name *Dirty Red* or call it *Black Gold* or *Texas Tea*, but as promised, Daddy, I will get it done. I have some of the stories you recorded with me, and with Mommy's help—and hopefully if I find Uncle Otis' recording—readers will read about the despicable plight formerly enslaved Penny Parson (as well as other formally enslaved African Americans) endured, and the generations born free after Penny and King Parson's emancipation—the same day, August 2nd, 1870.

I know you—as well as mommy—have always been proud of me and my sisters. This will just be another part of our family legacy to savor. This book is as much for you as it is for Grandpa Jesse's legacy. It's our family's legacy—your legacy—and we'll make sure it's never forgotten

As Reginald Satterfield always said:

"*Strike While the Iron is Hot*"

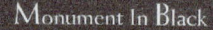

Monument In Black

Place my mother upon the penny
With the smile she held for me
Let the scares of troublesome reveal
The struggles she bore to be free

Carve my father in a nickel
Let his strength and pride remain
Put the works he did for our people
On exhibit, in the hall of fame.

Make a monument of my grandparents
Let it stand in Washington DC
Keep strait the trail they left behind
And to follow are you and me.

Pay a tribute to my brother,
On a peaceful day in June
For he was fighting in a war
Now lies restless in his
Star-Spangled tomb

Monica Regina Satterfield, © 1985

FORWARD

Duane's Tee Time Tales is an extraordinary and unexpected blend of civil rights history and untold family stories inspired by real-life events. As family to the characters—someone who lived through the era and witnessed various scenes—I know firsthand the immense value this book offers to readers of all generations. Whether you are a golfer, a historian, or a romantic at heart, this story holds both educational and entertainment value, taking readers on an unforgettable journey of love, and legacy.

If we, as African Americans, don't share our stories with one another and open them up to curious minds, we risk leaving our history vulnerable to inaccuracies—or worse, to silence. Ancestors of these characters took great pride in families and unity, and I am deeply honored to reflect on the remarkable life of one such man: Jesse Satterfield. Not only was he a hardworking man of unwavering integrity, but he also passed down one of the most endearing qualities—the art of being a provider—to his son, my husband of 65 years, the late and great Reginald "Red" Satterfield, who is among the characters depicted in this book.

Jesse Satterfield grew up without his mother, but he was lovingly raised by his grandparents Samantha and Samuel Satterfield. During that time and long before, African Americans relied on one another to learn, grow, and enrich their lives. Access to encyclopedias, let alone the internet or social media, was scarce, and our stories were preserved through oral traditions, handwritten inscriptions in family Bibles, and careful repetition of history from one generation to the next. It was through these labors of love in storytelling that our legacy survived—and this book carries that tradition forward, offering a meaningful gift to the next generation.

Duane's Tee Time Tales honors our ancestors' determination and sacrifices, crafting a narrative that is poignant, powerful and some chapters imaginative for the purpose of storytelling. Whether you're seeking history, entertainment, indulging in curiosity, or simply offering your support, I wholeheartedly encourage my family and yours to dive into this beautifully written expository historical fiction novel. It is a testament to the strength of our family, the importance of history, and the enduring pride of a people who refused to let their stories be forgotten.

Congratulations and thank you Duane and Monica. You have made our family proud of the Satterfield name.

With all my love
2025 Barbara Jean Satterfield

The Time

The road through fairways on golf courses for African Americans—once widely referred to as *Negros*, later *Colored People*, *Blacks*, now *African Americans*—was not fair at all. At one time, our people were limited to playing the sport only at certain local municipal parks, where they could access designated courses solely on specific days—spaces reserved for Negros or *Coloreds* use under restricted conditions. Despite the achievements of Black golfers, documented as early as the 1920s, African Americans were excluded from PGA events due to racism well into the mid-20th century. A separate tournament for African American golfers had to be established in 1928, thus the creation of the United Golfer Association by Robert Hawkins. Reportedly just two years after Black History Week was established.[1] While intercollegiate golf was born in the late 1800's, golf was largely considered a sport for elite and affluent white students dominated by ivy league colleges. Similarly, African Americans in the sport of golf at large, lagged way behind African Americans in other sports due to deep racism in the United States.[2]

Before the false notion of "separate-but-equal" was legally dismantled, the United States sanctioned segregation laws that claimed racial separation was fair. In reality, segregation was anything but equal—it divided people based on race, with glaring disparities between the treatment of races. The assertion that separation could ever be fair and equal violates the "Equal Protection Clause" of the Constitution.[3]

Consider, for example, White people in the United States traveling across the Atlantic Ocean at will, able to visit the continent of Africa to enrich themselves and return home to the United States. White passengers on these ships traveled freely. In stark contrast, well into the 19th century, if the human crossing the Atlantic was Colored, the experience was drastically different.

Grab'em! Drag'em away from their tribe! Choke hold'em into chains around their neck and feet! These Africans were thrown like cargo in a lower deck. Toilets? No! Like cattle standing in urine, feces and vomit, *Colored* folk were piled into a cargo area, one on top of one another, covered in shared excrement with no access to fresh air.

These *separate* areas were often on the same ships that the Whites and Europeans traveled by. They were separated on the ship according to race; separate but very clearly not equal. Whites and Colored remained separated from the moment they embarked on the same ship and journeyed the across the Atlantic. Once the *Negro human* stepped onto American soil, that person was immediately placed on an auction block inside a market, sold to another human, and forced into labor, tortured and terrorized for generations.

Separate-but-equal was always a lie because it was based on the humans' race. *Separate* meant descendants of humans who journeyed as captives, became enslaved persons in *separate* ship quarters, and fought with Union soldiers in America's Civil War— later declared free and forever woven and indelibly recorded into America's history—are ordered to eat, drink and play in and on separate recreational facilities, ordered through laws called 'doctrines' of segregation. Segregation meant the colored person, called *Negro*, was educated in different schools and used different parks and courses for golf or tennis. The laws of Segregation did not allow 'Colored' people, 'Negros,' 'Blacks,' or 'African Americans' to access to the same things as 'Whites'.

There are numerous definitions for racism. The term doesn't just come down to synonyms like discrimination, segregation, or prejudice. It is a fundamentally wrong and wicked belief that some humans are superior while other humans are inferior based on human 'biological'— and often physical—traits such as race, ethnicity, nationality. The CDC highlights in numerous reports racism as a public threat and health crisis. Racism is a wickedness that not only breeds behaviors but also systems, which result in disadvantages that carry increased risks of diseases. Racisms is factual and historic, a cause-and-effect issue that must be recognized and acknowledged to eliminate.

Whether golf originated in the 1300's by the Chinese or in the 1500's by the Scottish, historians agree the game crossed the Atlantic, making its way toward America, in the 1600's and by the mid 1700's a slave trader received the first shipment of golf equipment. [4]

Historians also agree that the PGA barred Negros from PGA golf tours, and point to provision of an organized tour for Negro golfers through creation of the United Golf Association.

Historians acknowledge that legendary boxer Joe Louis played a significant role in integrating golf. In 1952, Louis was allowed to compete in a PGA-sanctioned event, although he participated as an amateur and the event was not governed by PGA rules. At the time, the PGA had yet to fully include Black golfers; on the very day Louis played, another African American golfer was denied entry into the tournament. This exclusion did not go unnoticed by Louis, who likened the PGA to Nazis, putting additional pressure on the organization. Reports indicate that Louis told the *New York Times* and the *Los Angeles Sentinel*, "We've got another Hitler to get by."[5]

Despite his efforts, it would take another 38 years—until 1990—for the PGA to admit its first African American member, Ron Townsend. Moreover, it was not until 2012 that a woman, former U.S. Secretary of State Condoleezza Rice, became a member.[5]

Though many African Americans played golf—notably those of financial and social prominence—African Americans were often required to play in separate tournaments and on different golf courses. In some cases, they were only permitted on certain courses on specific days. L. J. Williams reported in the Negro History Bulletin in 1949 "young Negro boys were widely for as caddies," and learned the game and techniques later "becoming great Negro golfers of today."[6] During those days African Americans also had to organize their own golf leagues and tournaments. One of the two early golf tournaments that occurred in the 1940's for "Negros" was sponsored by legendary boxer Sugar Ray Robinson in New York yearly,[6] (not to be confused with Sugar Ray Leonard, a later boxer who modeled himself after Robinson). However, Negros aspired to play on equal footing, recognized for their skill rather than being segregated by race.

While historians eloquently memorialize golfing history for African Americans across the country, historical accounts of African Americans in golf overlooked an immediate and swift victory achieved by San Antonians following Thurgood Marshall's landmark argument against Jim Crow laws. Thurgood Marshall, then chief counsel of the National Association for the Advancement of Colored People, ("NAACP"), successfully argued in *Brown vs. Board of Education*—a name given to five separate cases—that separate-but-equal laws violated the Equal Protection Clause of the 14th Amendment, leading to the defeat of segregation in 1954.[3]

In 1953, the United States Supreme Court was initially divided over the issue of public-school segregation, reflecting the deeply entrenched nature of racial divisions across the country. Yet, by 1954, a transformative and unanimous decision was reached, one that would forever reshape the landscape of American civil rights. In the *Brown v. Board of Education* decision, delivered on May 17, 1954, Chief Justice Earl Warren, who had meticulously worked to bring together the differing opinions of the Justices, declared the doctrine of 'separate but equal' inherently unconstitutional within the realm of public education.[3] Warren's resolute words resounded throughout the country: "We conclude that in the field of public education the doctrine of 'separate but equal' has no place."[3] This landmark ruling not only struck down segregation in public schools but ignited a wave of civil rights advancements across various public domains, challenging long-standing racial barriers in every corner of American life.

Less than two weeks after this historic Supreme Court decision, another significant, albeit lesser-known, event unfolded in San Antonio, Texas. On May 25, 1954, just nine days after the *Brown v. Board* ruling, African Americans in San Antonio, empowered by the legal precedent, swiftly mobilized to demand equal access to the city's public golf courses—specifically the historic Brackenridge Golf Course, as well as Riverside and Willow Springs. The City Clerk, Mayor and City Council of San Antonio Texas received the petition submitted by citizens of San Antonio Negro Golfers' Association, requesting privileges of local municipal golf courses.[7] Following the petition, the City Council of San Antonio first adopted a resolution presenting it is a memorial on June 17, 1954—which was passed and approved the same day.[15a] Therein the City Council of San Antonio recognized African Americans' commitment to the United States of America in their service in the last two major World Wars and the Korean War referring to their service as "gallant deeds" having then being "indelibly recorded." Furthermore, the City Council recognized African Americans as patriots having paid the supreme sacrifice thereby "Obliterating the concept of [f]irst, second and third class citizens," thereby "ushering in a new social landscape rooting out discrimination the practice of equality as set out in our Declaration of Independence should become a reality." The city's segregation ordinance, which had enforced a practice of separate playing days for "Negro and White races" on municipally owned golf courses, was swiftly overturned starting with two resolutions declaring:

1. "The all municipally owned and operated golf courses facilities shall be open completely, without any restrictions to any user because of color, creed, or racial extraction, to the full use and enjoyment by all citizens.

2. That is further resolved that we disapprove of discrimination against any American."[15a]

The speed with which African Americans in San Antonio petitioned their city, and the decisive response, signaled a remarkable commitment to ending segregation in public spaces.

A special meeting of the City Council of the City of San Antonio was held in the council chambers of the City Hall on Saturday June 19th, 1954. A resolution by the City Council of San Antonio was read which wrote the following:

"Whereas it has been the custom of the city of San Antonio for many years that the use of public recreational facilities be enjoyed by the citizens of San Antonio on a segregated basis, and

"Whereas application has been made to persons of the Negro race to abolish the segregated use of the City recreational facilities in certain cases, and

"Whereas the present City Council of San Antonio is sympathetic with the wishes to treat all of the citizens of San Antonio in a fair and equitable manner now and therefore be it resolved by the City Council of San Antonio of the San Antonio that the use of all city-owned golf courses and tennis courts shall be hereafter open to and shall be enjoyed by all citizens of the City of San Antonio on an unsegregated bases." The Resolution was passed and approved June 19, 1954. [15 b,c]

Just five days later, on June 22, 1954, Jesse Satterfield and Sgt. Edward Green made history by becoming the first two African Americans (male or female) to officially play on the prestigious Brackenridge Golf Course. [16, 17] This momentous occasion was documented by local newspapers, further cementing the event's historical significance, even though the formal ordinance ratifying the changes wasn't officially documented until March 22, 1956. Nevertheless, San Antonio had already made its mark in history as a pioneering city in the fight for civil rights, standing in tandem with the winds of change initiated by *Brown v. Board of Education.*

In stark contrast, the fight to desegregate public golf courses in other southern cities, such as Atlanta, Georgia, progressed at a much slower pace. Atlanta did not follow San Antonio's example nor the spirit of the *Brown v. Board* decision with the same urgency. It wasn't until November 7, 1955—nearly a year and a half after *Brown*—that public golf courses in Atlanta, Georgia were desegregated. This change came only after a federal lawsuit was filed by civil rights activists Charles Bell, Tup Holmes, and Oliver Holmes—under a lawsuit named *Holmes v. Atlanta*—who courageously challenged the city's entrenched segregationist policies.[11] Atlanta's delayed response highlights the varied pace at which different regions of the United States embraced the dismantling of segregation, underscoring the unique and trailblazing role San Antonio, Texas played in this pivotal period of civil rights history. According to historians Norman Shavin and Bruce Galpin: "the first scene of court-ordered desegregation in Georgia was a golf course and not a schoolhouse[.]"[18]

The Supreme Court's ruling in *Holmes*, which followed the *Brown* decision, played a pivotal role in this change. Mr. Holmes, having been denied access to public golf courses, initiated the lawsuit, with the NAACP and Thurgood Marshall contributing to the case's successful outcome in the 1955 Supreme Court decision. As a result, it wasn't until December 24 and 25, 1955, that the trio—Tup Holmes, Oliver Holmes, and Charles Bell—actually played on the desegregated golf courses, effectively ending segregation in Georgia.[9,10,11,18] While this event was monumental and deserving of recognition, it nevertheless occurred 18 months after the swift response seen in San Antonio, where Jesse Satterfield and Sgt. Edward Green broke the color barrier at Texas' historic golf courses. Unfortunately, these significant events have not been publicly celebrated.

Despite San Antonio's notable achievement, the contributions of African Americans in desegregating its golf courses were overlooked in a *People* magazine article written in honor of Texas' Hall of Fame golf course, Brackenridge, during its 100-year celebration. The article highlights various historical milestones, including how Brackenridge was the first course in San Antonio to encourage women to play, and how it made golf more accessible with lower green fees. It also acknowledges the inclusion of Mexican Americans in the 1960s but fails to mention the groundbreaking efforts of African Americans in desegregating the course—an accomplishment that both the state of Texas and the city of San Antonio should proudly commemorate. The article specifically states, "In its early years, the group faced some discrimination, even at the public course where it held tournaments. Mexican Americans weren't invited to play in city-sponsored amateur events, and the group was required to pre-pay rental fees. That changed by the 1960s."[12].

However, Brackenridge Park missed a critical opportunity to highlight a significant chapter of African American cultural history during its 100th and 125th anniversary celebrations—an oversight that diminishes the park's claim to being "steeped in history and culture."[24] The historic 100-year celebration, in particular, presented a perfect moment to reflect on San Antonio's progressive stance following the landmark *Brown v. Board of Education* decision. At a time when much of the country was resisting integration, San Antonio's City Council demonstrated leadership by passing desegregation legislation that sought to "treat all of the citizens of San Antonio in a fair and equitable manner."[15b,c] These laws ended the discriminatory practice of only allowing African Americans—then referred to as "Coloreds"—to play on certain days at city golf courses, including Brackenridge. The momentous occasion, documented in local newspapers, could have been a source of pride for both the park and the city, aligning its history with broader national progress.

Yet, this pivotal chapter of history was relegated to an obscure mention on pages 546 and 548 of the 576-page *Brackenridge Park Cultural Landscape Report.*[23] Even as the park celebrated its 125th anniversary 2024 with a yearlong campaign in 2024, touting itself as an "unparalleled blend of nature, culture, and history,"[24] it again failed to elevate the story of the courageous petitioners, Ste. Green and Mr. Jesse Satterfield, who broke the color barrier at Brackenridge. Instead of amplifying their contributions and the park's evolution during a time of profound social change, this history was buried and overlooked.

How could such a profound moment of progress—one that aligned with San Antonio's proud legacy of fairness and equity—be ignored in both milestone celebrations? By failing to recognize and highlight the park's role in desegregation, Brackenridge not only missed an opportunity to celebrate the trailblazing efforts of African American golfers but also did a disservice to history itself. Erasing, failing to recognize, or understating such monumental moments of change is, in itself, a disservice to history. Recognizing and honoring these stories is essential, not only to preserve the truth but also to inspire future generations with the legacy of resilience and progress.

In stark contrast, Atlanta honored its desegregation history by renaming a city golf course after Alfred "Tup" Holmes, recognizing his contributions to the desegregation of golf. The *Holmes* case was one of the first to extend the legal precedent set by *Brown v. Board of Education* beyond education and into other public accommodations, having an immediate and lasting impact.

The city of San Antonio should take inspiration from Austin, Texas, where the bravery of its citizens and the history of desegregation have been fully acknowledged. Several years before *Brown v. Board of*

Education, numerous cases challenged the Jim Crow laws of "separate but equal." Entire separate schools, including law schools, were created exclusively for Blacks, "Coloreds," and "Negros" because they were barred from attending schools for Whites. In the late 1940s, cases challenging the "separate but equal" doctrine were brought before the Supreme Court, paving the way for African Americans to attend law schools. By the summer of 1950, just days after the *Sweatt v. Painter* decision, African Americans applied to and were admitted into the University of Texas Law School.[13]

Historians in Austin have chronicled the city's pioneering role in desegregating golf courses within the Old Confederacy. They highlight the peaceful defiance that characterized this transition, often naming Alvin Propps, a nine-year-old caddie at Muny Municipal Golf Course, as a key figure in this historic achievement. The "Grounds for Democracy" article proudly acknowledges Austin's desegregation of public facilities prior to the *Brown v. Board* decision. The article also acknowledges the decision not to prosecute young Propps and his friend for playing golf at Muny without permission, in defiance of Jim Crow laws. The article goes on to even acknowledge the decision and lack of recognition as "an important advance in the history of U.S. civil rights, it has not always been recognized as such."[14]

San Antonio's historical significance in the desegregation of golf has failed to fully recognize its own legacy. Milestones in civil rights and forward steps toward progress should not be omitted, overlooked, or understated. When Brackenridge Golf Course celebrated its 100th anniversary, there was an opportunity to honor and embrace the African American history tied to it, but the local news failed to do so. The city of San Antonio, its surrounding community, and golf historians should acknowledge Mr. Jesse Satterfield not only as a trailblazer but also as a former employee of Willow Springs Golf Course, which was affiliated with Brackenridge and managed by the same nonprofit group. Dedicating a memorial or renaming a section of the golf course in honor of Mr. Jesse Satterfield, Sgt. Green, and the San Antonio petitioners would not only celebrate their enduring legacy but also ensure their significant contributions are preserved. This act would provide future generations with the opportunity to honor, learn from, and be inspired by their remarkable achievements and steadfast dedication to equality and progress.

Therefore, as part of a tribute to Mr. Jesse Satterfield, Sgt. Green, and the San Antonio petitioners who helped desegregate San Antonio's public golf courses, *Duane's Tee Time Tales and Historic Fairway* is written as expository fiction. Thus, the historic details used for this introduction are factual and the science in these tales is grounded in reality, as honoring these pioneers and their historic achievements comes naturally. Mr. Jesse Satterfield, Sgt. Green, and the ninety-seven San Antonio petitioners' efforts paved the way for a more inclusive and equitable future in the sport of golf.

The following letter from the City Clerk was read:

Honorable Mayor and Members of Council
City of San Antonio, Texas

Gentlemen:

The following petitions were received by this office and referred to Mr. Ralph
H. Winton, City Manager, for his recommendation or action.

5-25-54   Petition of Most Rev. Robert E. Lucey requesting tax exemption of Lots
          28, 29, 30, New City Block 8341

5-25-54   Petition of San Antonio Negro Golfers' Association requesting golfing
          privileges of local municipal golf courses.

June 17, 1954

REGULAR MEETING OF THE CITY COUNCIL
OF THE CITY OF SAN ANTONIO HELD IN
THE COUNCIL CHAMBER OF THE CITY HALL
ON THURSDAY, JUNE 17, 1954 AT 10:00 A.M.

PRESENT: Scherlen, Stevens, Shearer, Russell, Easley, Lester, Gonzalez

ABSENT: A. C. White, R. N. White   Mayor Pro-tem R. L. Lester presiding.

Invocation by Mr. Scherlen.

On motion of Mr. Russell, seconded by Mr. Gonzalez, the reading of the minutes of the previous meeting was dispensed with.

-           -   -

The following ordinance was passed and approved by the following vote:
Ayes, Scherlen, Stevens, Shearer, Russell, Easley, Lester, Gonzalez. Nays, none; absent, A. C. White, R. N. White.

AN ORDINANCE 20,288

AN ORDINANCE TO USE THE CITY SANITARY SEWERS BY
A CONNECTION OUTSIDE OF THE CITY LIMITS ON THE
PETITION OF MR. F. K. STEGER AT 500 MORNINGSIDE

(Full text in Ordinance Book AA page 79)

-           -   -

The following ordinance was passed and approved by the following vote:
Ayes, Scherlen, Stevens, Shearer, Russell, Easley, Lester, Gonzalez; Nays, none; Absent, A. C. White, R. N. White.

AN ORDINANCE 20,289

AN ORDINANCE TO USE THE CITY SANITARY SEWERS BY A
CONNECTION OUTSIDE OF THE CITY LIMITS ON THE PETITION
OF WALTER LEISE AT 600 RITTIMAN ROAD

(Full text in Ordinance Book AA page 80)

-           -   -

The following ordinance was passed and approved by the following vote:
Ayes, Scherlen, Stevens, Shearer, Russell, Easley, Lester, Gonzalez; Nays, none; Absent, A. C. White, R. N. White.

AN ORDINANCE 20,290

AN ORDINANCE TO USE THE CITY SANITARY SEWERS BY A
CONNECTION OUTSIDE OF THE CITY LIMITS ON THE PETITION
OF MR. & MRS. O. C. COMPTON AT 134 GITTINGER

(Full text in Ordinance Book AA page 80)

-           -   -

The following ordinance was passed and approved by the following vote:
Ayes, Scherlen, Stevens, Shearer, Russell, Easley, Lester, Gonzalez; Nays, none; Absent, A. C. White, R. N. White.

AN ORDINANCE 20,291

AN ORDINANCE TO USE THE CITY SANITARY SEWERS BY A
CONNECTION OUTSIDE OF THE CITY LIMITS ON THE PETITION
OF LEON W. LUKSA AT 219 SUNNY CREST

(Full text in Ordinance Book AA page 80)

The following ordinance was passed and approved by the following vote: Ayes, Scherlen, Stevens, Shearer, Russell, Easley, Lester, Gonzalez; Nays, none; Absent, A. C. White, R. N. White.

AN ORDINANCE 20,292

AN ORDINANCE TO USE THE CITY SANITARY SEWERS BY
A CONNECTION OUTSIDE OF THE CITY LIMITS ON THE
PETITION OF CLARENCE THORNE AT 134 CITY VIEW

(Full text in Ordinance Book AA page 81)

The following ordinance was passed and approved by the following vote: Ayes, Scherlen, Stevens, Shearer, Russell, Easley, Lester, Gonzalez; Nays, none; Absent, A. C. White, R. N. White.

AN ORDINANCE 20,293

AN ORDINANCE TO USE THE CITY SANITARY SEWERS BY
A CONNECTION OUTSIDE OF THE CITY LIMITS ON THE
PETITION OF S. POGUE AT 1313 WILTSHIRE

(Full text in Ordinance Book AA page 81)

The following ordinance was passed and approved by the following vote: Ayes, Scherlen, Stevens, Shearer, Russell, Easley, Lester, Gonzalez; Nays, none; Absent, A. C. White, R. N. White.

AN ORDINANCE 20,294

AN ORDINANCE TO USE THE CITY SANITARY SEWERS BY
A CONNECTION OUTSIDE OF THE CITY LIMITS ON THE
PETITION OF E. B. GARCIA AT SAMS DRIVE

(Full text in Ordinance Book AA page 81)

The following ordinance was passed and approved by the following vote: Ayes, Scherlen, Stevens, Shearer, Russell, Easley, Lester, Gonzalez; Nays, none; Absent, A. C. White, R. N. White.

AN ORDINANCE 20,295

AMENDING CHAPTER 60, ARTICLE 4, ENTITLED "PARKING"
OF THE SAN ANTONIO CITY CODE BY ADDING AND INCLUDING
A NEW SECTION WHICH DESIGNATES AREAS PERMITTING PARALLEL
PARKING ONLY AND DESIGNATED AS SECTION 60-55.1 ENTITLED
"PARALLEL PARKING ONLY"

(Full text in Ordinance Book AA page 81)

The following ordinance was passed and approved by the following vote: Ayes, Scherlen, Stevens, Shearer, Russell, Easley, Lester, Gonzalez; Nays, none; Absent, A. C. White, R. N. White.

AN ORDINANCE 20,296

ACCEPTING THE PROPOSED CONTRACT OF FRIDEN CAL-
CULATING MACHINE AGENCY FOR THE SERVICING OF
FOURTEEN (14) CALCULATING MACHINES FOR A PERIOD
OF ONE (1) YEAR ENDING NOVEMBER 6, 1954, AT A
TOTAL COST OF $452.28

(Full text in Ordinance Book AA page 82)

The following ordinance was passed and approved by the following vote:
Ayes, Scherlen, Stevens, Shearer, Russell, Easley, Lester, Gonzalez; Nays, none; Absent,
A. C. White, R. N. White.

AN ORDINANCE 20,297

AUTHORIZING THE CITY MANAGER TO ENTER INTO A LEASE
AGREEMENT WITH THE TEXAS HIGHWAY DEPARTMENT, FOR
RENTAL OF A CITY-OWNED BUILDING AT 520 WEST ELMIRA
STREET, FOR A TERM OF FOUR YEARS

(Full text in Ordinance Book AA page 83)

The following resolution was passed and approved by the following vote:
Ayes, Scherlen, Stevens, Shearer, Russell, Easley, Lester, Gonzalez; Nays, none; Absent,
A. C. White, R. N. White.

A RESOLUTION

AUTHORIZING THE CITY MANAGER TO MAKE APPLICATION
TO THE STATE DEFENSE AND DISASTER RELIEF OFFICIALS
TO SECURE MATCHING FUNDS ON A FIFTY-FIFTY BASIS FROM
THE FEDERAL CIVIL DEFENSE ADMINISTRATION TO PURCHASE
ADDITIONAL AIR RAID WARNING EQUIPMENT, IN THE AMOUNT
OF APPROXIMATELY $97,000.00 TO BE USED IN THE LOCAL
CIVIL DEFENSE PROGRAM

(Full text in Ordinance Book AA page 82)

The following ordinance was passed and approved by the following vote:
Ayes, Scherlen, Stevens, Shearer, Russell, Easley, Lester, Gonzalez; Nays, none; Absent,
A. C. White, R. N. White.

AN ORDINANCE 20,298

ACCEPTING THE PROPOSAL OF R. J. JEFFERDS TO
PREPARE AND SERVICE ALL VOTING MACHINES TO
BE USED IN THE ELECTION ON JULY 10, 1954

(Full text in Ordinance Book AA page 83)

The following ordinance was passed and approved by the following vote:
Ayes, Scherlen, Stevens, Shearer, Russell, Easley, Lester, Gonzalez; Nays, none; Absent,
A. C. White, R. N. White.

AN ORDINANCE 20,299

ACCEPTING THE PROPOSAL OF TALLEY TRANSFER
COMPANY FOR THE TRANSPORTATION OF VOTING MACHINES
FOR THE ELECTION TO BE HELD ON JULY 10, 1954

(Full text in Ordinance Book AA page 84)

The following ordinance was passed and approved by the following vote:
Ayes, Scherlen, Stevens, Shearer, Russell, Easley, Lester, Gonzalez; Nays, none; Absent,
A. C. White, R. N. White.

AN ORDINANCE 20,300

MAKING A CONTRACT WITH THE COUNTY OF BEXAR
FOR RENTAL OF VOTING MACHINES

(Full text in Ordinance Book AA page 84)

The following ordinance was passed and approved by the following vote: Ayes, Scherlen, Stevens, Shearer, Russell, Easley, Lester, Gonzalez; Nays, none; Absent, A. C. White, R. N. White.

AN ORDINANCE 20,301

EXTENDING THE PERIOD OF CONTRACT WITH G. C. WOLFE, JR., TO TAKE WATER FROM MITCHELL LAKE FOR IRRIGATION PURPOSES, FOR ONE YEAR, FROM MAY 1, 1954 TO APRIL 30, 1955

(Full text in Ordinance Book AA page 85)

-                    -   -

The following ordinance was passed and approved by the following vote: Ayes, Scherlen, Stevens, Shearer, Russell, Easley, Lester, Gonzalez; Nays, none; Absent, A. C. White, R. N. White.

AN ORDINANCE 20,302

CHANGING THE NAMES OF CERTAIN STREETS LOCATED WITHIN THE CITY OF SAN ANTONIO

(Full text in Ordinance Book AA page 86)

-                    -   -

The following resolution was passed and approved by the following vote: Ayes, Scherlen, Stevens, Shearer, Russell, Easley, Lester, Gonzalez; Nays, none; Absent, A. C. White, R. N. White.

A RESOLUTION

GIVING NOTICE OF A PUBLIC HEARING OF A PROPOSED AMENDMENT TO THE ORDINANCE ESTABLISHING ZONING REGULATIONS AND DISTRICTS, ETC., PASSED AND APPROVED ON NOVEMBER 3, 1938, BY CHANGING THE CLASSIFICATION DESCRIBED HEREIN (CASE NOS. 374, 377, 378 - HEARING TO BE HELD JULY 8, 1954)

-                    -   -

The following ordinance was passed and approved by the following vote: Ayes, Scherlen, Stevens, Shearer, Russell, Easley, Lester, Gonzalez; Nays, none; Absent, A. C. White, R. N. White.

AN ORDINANCE 20,303

AMENDING SECTION 2 OF AN ORDINANCE ENTITLED "AN ORDINANCE ESTABLISHING ZONING REGULATIONS AND DISTRICTS IN ACCORDANCE WITH A COMPREHENSIVE PLAN, ETC," PASSED AND APPROVED ON NOVEMBER 3, 1938, BY CHANGING THE CLASSIFICATION AND RE-ZONING OF CERTAIN PROPERTY DESCRIBED HEREIN

(Full text in Ordinance Book AA page 86)

-                    -   -

The following resolution was passed and approved by the following vote: Ayes, Scherlen, Stevens, Shearer, Russell, Easley, Lester, Gonzalez; Nays, none; Absent, A. C. White, R. N. White.

A RESOLUTION

AUTHORIZING AND DIRECTING THE CITY CLERK TO ADVERTISE FOR BIDS FOR THE SALVAGE RIGHTS AT ALL CITY DUMPS FOR A PERIOD OF ONE YEAR

The following ordinance was passed and approved by the following vote: Ayes, Scherlen, Stevens, Shearer, Russell, Easley, Lester, Gonzalez; Nays, none; Absent, A. C. White, R. N. White.

AN ORDINANCE 20,304

AMENDING SECTION 41-4, AS AMENDED JULY 10, 1952, OF THE SAN ANTONIO CITY CODE PERTAINING TO THE DISCHARGE OF WATER OR ANY FLUID ON OR INTO CITY STREETS

(Full text in Ordinance Book AA page 87)

-            -   -

The following ordinance was passed and approved by the following vote: Ayes, Scherlen, Stevens, Shearer, Russell, Easley, Lester, Gonzalez; Nays, none; Absent, A. C. White, R. N. White.

AN ORDINANCE 20,305

AMENDING SECTION 2 OF AN ORDINANCE ENTITLED "AN ORDINANCE ESTABLISHING ZONING REGULATIONS AND DISTRICTS IN ACCORDANCE WITH A COMPREHENSIVE PLAN, ETC." PASSED AND APPROVED ON NOVEMBER 3, 1938, BY CHANGING THE CLASSIFICATION AND RE-ZONING OF CERTAIN PROPERTY DESCRIBED HEREIN; AND REPEALING ORDINANCE NO. 20,282, PASSED AND APPROVED ON THE 10TH DAY OF JUNE,1954

(Full text in Ordinance Book AA page 87)

-            -   -

The following ordinance was passed and approved by the following vote: Ayes, Scherlen, Stevens, Shearer, Russell, Easley, Lester, Gonzalez; Nays, none; Absent, A. C. White, R. N. White.

AN ORDINANCE 20,306

AUTHORIZING THE CITY MANAGER TO EXECUTE TRANSFER AGREEMENT ON BEHALF OF THE CITY OF SAN ANTONIO WITH THE COUNTY OF PRESIDIO, TEXAS

(Full text in Ordinance Book AA page 88)

-            -   -

The following resolution was passed and approved by the following vote: Ayes, Scherlen, Stevens, Shearer, Russell, Easley, Lester, Gonzalez; Nays, none; Absent, A. C. White, R. N. White.

A RESOLUTION

EXPRESSING THE INTENT ON THE PART OF THE CITY COUNCIL TO FURTHER INVESTIGATE AND STUDY THE MOST FEASIBLE ROUTE TO BE DESIGNATED FOR EXPRESSWAY U. S. HIGHWAY 87 NORTH

(Full text in Ordinance Book AA page 88)

-            -   -

The following letter from the City Clerk was read:

Honorable Mayor and Members of Council
City of San Antonio, Texas

Gentlemen:

The following petitions were received by this office and referred to Mr. Ralph H. Winton, City Manager, for his recommendation or action.

6-9-54 Petition of Jay Sam Levey, in behalf of property owners in Monticello Heights Addition requesting the city to grade and gravel the alley between their properties between Babcock Road and Loma Linda.

6-9-54 Petition of K. M. Fisher for approval of transfer of forty taxicab permits or certificates of convenience and necessity to M. L. Fisher.

6-9-54   Petition of Mrs. Albertene Bonn requesting permission to close an alley in NCB 7800.

6-10-54 Petition of Rolla S. Taylor, Chairman State Association of Texas Pioneers, protesting against the Witte Museum for encroaching upon the recreation grounds in the rear of the Memorial Building.

6-10-54 Petition of Charles E. Muench protesting certain conditions in San Pedro Park.

6-10-54 Petition of Wayne McAfee, Trustee, Church of God, requesting tax exemption of Lots 1 to 10 incl., NCB 8249.

6-11-54 Petition of Home Mission Board of the Southern Baptist Convention requesting tax exemption of the middle one-third of Lot 35, Block 1, NCB 8725

6-14-54 Petition of Mrs. Elvira G. Benavides requesting the city to close, abandon and quit claim part of an alley in NCB 2909.

6-14-54 . Petition of Jimmy R. Flores, et al, requesting the repair of the 700, 800 and 900 blocks of Milvid Street.

6-14-54 Petition of Rudolph Rubin, Sr., et al, requesting that 30 mile per hour signs be placed on Sunshine Drive East, between Dickinson and St. Cloud Roads.

Yours very truly,

J. Frank Gallagher
City Clerk

Zoning Case #367 was next called up for a continued hearing after having been recessed. On the petition of William A. Bedell for rezoning property at southwest corner of San Pedro Avenue and Jackson Keller Road - Lot A3, NCB 10047 - from "A" Residential to "F" Local Retail. Mr. John Peace, Attorney for the petitioner, addressed the council and showed the aspects of the case by maps and charts, showing business encroaching and no possibility of this property being residential and the growth of the area beyond making the change advisable. No one appeared in protest but a petition had previously been filed with the Clerk purporting to contain names of owners of 20% of the immediate adjacent property owners thus necessitating a vote of 3/4 of the council "in esse" for approval. Mr. Shearer disqualified himself because of personal interest in adjacent property making the number of votes necessary to approve, 6.

On motion of Mr. Scherlen, seconded by Mr. Gonzalez, the recommendation of the Planning Commission was approved by the following vote: Ayes, Scherlen, Stevens, Russell, Easley, Lester, and Gonzalez; Nays, none; Absent, A. C. White, R. N. White; Disqualified, Shearer.

Zoning Case #371 to rezone property on Hildebrand Avenue, which was recessed from last week, was next called. Mr. Ben Lucas, representing the petitioner appeared and stated he did not see need for further taking time of the council since the case was thoroughly discussed last week. Mrs. J. V. Cook appeared again, as did Mr. Steele and others. After discussion, a motion by Mr. Scherlen, seconded by Mr. Shearer to approve the recommendation of the Planning Board to rezone this property failed passage by the following vote: Ayes, Scherlen, Shearer, Lester; Nays, Stevens, Easley, Gonzalez. Absent, A. C. White, R. N. White; Disqualified, Russell.

Mr. Gonzalez next asked for permission to read the following three resolutions:

AN ORDINANCE

CREATING A COMMISSION FOR COMMUNITY
INTERRELATIONS

BE IT ORDAINED BY THE CITY COUNCIL OF THE CITY OF SAN ANTONIO:

Section 1. That there is hereby created a Commission of fifteen members, all residents of the City of San Antonio, to be known as the COMMISSION FOR COMMUNITY INTERRELATIONS.

Section 2. The members of this commission shall be appointed by the City Manager subject to the approval of the City Council, the members of this Commission being appointed to a term of office not to exceed two years. The members of this Commission shall be appointed as nearly as practicable from the various sections of the City so as to represent a cross section of the community.

Section 3. This Commission shall be primarily created for the purpose of evolving a constructive pattern of community interrelations.

PASSED AND APPROVED this 17th day of June, A. D. 1954.

RESOLUTION OF THE CITY COUNCIL
OF SAN ANTONIO, ADOPTED AS A
RESOLUTION, AND PRESENTED AS A
MEMORIAL TO CITIZENS AND INTERESTED
OFFICIALS

CONSIDERING:

The City of San Antonio, like all cities of America, is composed of persons of all racial backgrounds, creeds, and religions. All have lived in peace and harmony to a far greater extend than in less happier communities, for which all God-fearing citizens than our Lord Creator for his Grace thus shed upon us and our City. San Antonio as whole has worked towards the goal of equalizing opportunity for all, irrespective of race, color or creed, using always the tradional American democratic processes to realize this ideal.

In two major world wars within the past thirty seven years, every able bodied citizen, regardless of race, color or creed was called upon to serve his country. The gallant deeds performed by those men, in particular, of the Negro race, are now indelibly recorded. In the Korean war, not too long ago terminated, their record of achievement was the same. Outstanding among our patriots, many of whom made the supreme sacrifice, are those, called by some, of the Negro race.

We are now calling attention to the recent Supreme Court decisions, reflecting the thinking of the great majority of our people, that are in effect obliterating the concept of First, second and third class citizens, except in war. Thus ushering in a new social landscape rooting out discrimination, the practice of the equality as set out in our Declaration of Independence should become a reality. Our challenge to the whole world must be fairness and equality and no discrimination for any people within our country.

NOW THEREFORE BE IT RESOLVED:

1. That all municipally owned and operated golf courses be opened completely, without any restrictions to any user because of color, creed, or racial extraction, to the full use and enjoyment by all citizens.

2. That it is further resolved that we disapprove of discrimination against any American.

AN ORDINANCE

CREATING A CITY FINANCE STUDY COMMISSION

BE IT ORDAINED BY THE CITY COUNCIL OF THE CITY OF SAN ANTONIO:

Section 1. That there is hereby created a Commission consisting of six members, all residents of the City of San Antonio, to be known as the City Finance Study Commission.

Section 2. The members of this Commission shall be appointed by the City Manager subject to the approval of the Council, the members of this Commission being appointed to a term of office not to exceed two years. It is expected that the persons thus chosen to serve shall be well versed and experienced in municipal, financial tax, or business matters.

Section 3. The increase of municipal services, with the resulting need for increased revenues to finance these activities, is the reason for the creation of this Commission.

The main purpose of the Commission shall be to weigh and analyze the various factors affecting San Antonio Municipal finances and taxes, in order to seek out ways and means of securing a broader revenue base.

****

After the reading, Mr. Russell moved that all three be laid on the table subject to call when the council meets in special session to consider the subjects referred to; seconded by Mrs. Stevens, the motion was carried: Ayes, Scherlen, Stevens, Shearer, Russell, Easley, Lester; Nays, none; Absent, A. C. White, R. N. White; Not voting, Gonzalez.

Mrs. Betty Aigner of 149 Smallwood Avenue addressed the council and read in person a lengthy petition complaining of lack of services and asking to be given full service or de-annexed. The petition containing 103 names was filed with the Clerk.

Mr. Seymour Flatow appeared before the council to protest a charge made for services to a non profit charitable organization. He claimed the fee quoted was $400.00 whereas the bill was $463.00. Mr. Sol Wolf, Manager of the Auditorium, explained the matter fully and the whole matter of auditorium rates was fully discussed. Mr. Easley made a motion to accept $400. and cancel the remaining $63.00. The motion was lost by the following vote: Ayes, Scherlen, Stevens, Easley, Lester; Nays, Shearer, Russell, Gonzalez; not being the necessary five votes.

Mr. Shearer then agreed to donate $63.00 to cerebral palsy fund to take care of the charge.

On motion of Mr. Russell, seconded by Mr. Gonzalez, the meeting adjourned.

APPROVED: *[signature]*

MAYOR

ATTEST:

[signature]
City Clerk

ADDENDUM

At the informal meeting of the council held in the City Manager's Office a letter from YMCA signed by Hector Diaz was read asking for a waiver of all permit fees in the construction of a YMCA building at 4955 W. Commerce. The Manager was instructed to issue an order waiving these fees.

　　　　－　　　　　　　　　　　－　　　　　　　　　　　　－

The question was brought up by Mr. Easley as to whether or not the route for Freeway, 87 North heretofore adopted was the best route. After discussion the City Attorney was instructed to draw a resolution calling for a further study of the matter.

　　　　－　　　　　　　　　　　－　　　　　　　　　　　　－

A letter from Howard T. Harris on the above subject was read by the Clerk.

　　　　－　　　　　　　　　　　－　　　　　　　　　　　　－

A letter from Mrs. Preston H. Dial, President of the Council of International Relations, asking for a scroll to be issued to Athanaseus Delikostopoulos as Alcalde of La Villita. The issuance was approved.

Mr. Russell moved that hereafter the Mayor or Mayor Pro-tem be allowed to use his judgment and issue such scroll as he deemed wise. All present agreed.

　　　　－　　　　　　　　　　　－　　　　　　　　　　　　－

A committee of citizens appeared in behalf of an ordinance to change the regulations regarding the washing of filling station driveways. After discussion it was decided to pass an amending ordinance.

SPECIAL MEETING OF THE CITY COUNCIL
OF THE CITY OF SAN ANTONIO HELD IN THE
COUNCIL CHAMBER OF THE CITY HALL AT
10:30 A.M., SATURDAY, JUNE 19, 1954

PRESENT: SCHERLEN, STEVENS, SHEARER, RUSSELL, EASLEY, LESTER, GONZALEZ

ABSENT: A. C. WHITE, R. N. WHITE

Mayor Pro-tem R. L. Lester presiding.

Invocation by Rev. C. W. Black, Mt. Zion First Baptist Church

The Clerk read the call of the meeting as follows:

Mr. J. Frank Gallagher
City Clerk
City of San Antonio, Texas

Dear Sir:

Under authority vested in me by the Charter of the City,
I hereby request that you call a Special Meeting of the City
Council, required for the good of the City of San Antonio to
convene at 10:30 A.M., June 19, 1954, in the Council Chamber
of the City Hall of the City of San Antonio.

Yours very truly,

/s/ R. L. Lester

Honorable Mayor and Members of Council
City of San Antonio, Texas

Gentlemen:

Pursuant to a written request filed by Mayor Pro-tem Lester
you are hereby called into a Special Session of the City Council
to be held in the City Council Chamber in the City Hall at 10:30
A.M. on the 19th day of June, 1954 for the good of the City.

Respectfully,

/s/ J. Frank Gallagher
City Clerk

Receipt of the above Special Meeting of the City Council of the
City of San Antonio is hereby acknowledged.

/s/ R. L. Lester   /s/ R. R. Russell, Jr.
/s/ H. J. Shearer   /s/ Ralph V. Easley
/s/ Thelma Stevens   /s/ Henry B. Gonzalez
/s/ Emil O. Scherlen

Mayor Pro-tem Lester, after calling the meeting to order, asked if there was
anyone in the audience wishing to be heard. Rev. C. W. Black responded and said that he
probably would like to address the council when he was sufficiently informed just what
was before the council.

Mr. Lester then introduced a resolution "pertaining to the furnishing of adequate
public park facilities for all citizens of San Antonio". The resolution was then discussed by Rev. Black, Dr. Ruth Bellinger, S. J. Sutton, Archie Johnson, and other leading
negro citizens. All protesting any legislation whatsoever regarding segregation of races.

After discussion by members of the Council the resolution was amended to read
as follows:

A RESOLUTION

BY THE CITY COUNCIL OF THE CITY OF SAN ANTONIO PER-
TAINING TO THE FURNISHING OF ADEQUATE PUBLIC PARK
FACILITIES FOR ALL OF THE CITIZENS OF SAN ANTONIO

WHEREAS, it has been the custom in the City of San Antonio for many years
that the use of public recreational facilities be enjoyed by the citizens of
San Antonio on a segregated basis, and

WHEREAS, application has been made by persons of the Negro race to
abolish the segregated use of City recreational facilities in certain
cases, and

WHEREAS, the present City Council of the City of San Antonio is sympathetic
with and wishes to treat all of the citizens of San Antonio in a fair and
equitable manner, now, therefore,

BE IT RESOLVED BY THE CITY COUNCIL OF THE CITY OF SAN ANTONIO:

     That the use of all city-owned golf courses and tennis courts shall be hereafter open to and shall be enjoyed by all citizens of the City of San Antonio on an unsegregated basis.

     PASSED AND APPROVED this 19th day of June, A. D. 1954.

                                R. L. Lester
                                Mayor Pro-tem

ATTEST:
J. Frank Gallagher
City Clerk

     The resolution was then passed by the following vote: Ayes, Scherlen, Stevens, Shearer, Russell, Easley, Lester, Gonzalez; Nays, none; Absent, A. C. White, R. N. White.

         -                 -   -

     Mr. Lester then introduced the following ordinance:

                     AN ORDINANCE 20,307

                  PROVIDING FOR THE SEGREGATION OF THE NEGRO AND WHITE RACES IN THE USE OF CERTAIN DESIGNATED CITY OPERATED RECREATION FACILITIES; PROVIDING A PENALTY FOR THE VIOLATION THEREOF AND DECLARING AN EMERGENCY

                  (Full text in Ordinance Book AA page 99)

     The matter was then thoroughly discussed by all the above mentioned negro citizens and others including Harry Burns and Menefee Dodson.

     Mr. Scherlen then addressed the council stating his opposition to its passage on grounds of unconstitutionality and morality. He does not believe the council has the right to pass such legislation. Mr. Gonzalez also registered his disapproval.

     Mrs. Stevens then called upon the City Manager for his recommendation regarding the ordinance. The Manager, Mr. Winton, made a statement direct to the negro citizens expressing to them his good will and his idea that he was not trying to work any hardship on them then turning to the council members he asked earnestly that the ordinance be passed. He feels that before opening the swimming pools, unsegregated, a transitional period is necessary and he asks that at least six members support the ordinance so that immediate effectiveness will follow. He cited his work heretofore for civil rights and friendliness to the negro race to show his sincerity but is firmly of the opinion that an educational period is necessary before wide open operation of pools.

     Several of the negro citizens replied direct to the City Manager, Mr. Winton. Mrs. Stevens and Mr. Easley both stated they would follow the wishes of the City Manager. The vote was taken and the ordinance was adopted by the following vote: Ayes, Stevens, Shearer, Russell, Easley and Lester; Nays, Scherlen, Gonzalez; Absent, A. C. White, R. N. White. There not being six votes the emergency clause was not effective.

         -                 -   -

     On motion of Mr. Russell, seconded by Mr. Easley, the meeting adjourned.

                        APPROVED: R. L. Lester

                                       MAYOR

ATTEST:

City Clerk

Part I

Made Perfect

In weakness our strength is made perfect
Not a body we built in a song
Nor a mind, through education despite the wrong
It's through infirmity; our spirits made forever strong

By combating the worthless liar
And removing that liar attacking self
From victory, to victory,
Each battle we won.
Our strength made perfect in
The Almighty's Son

In weakness our strength is made perfect
Through our battles our victories be made perfect
With His love, our spirit is made perfect
In God's eyes, we're a gift He made perfect!

PROLOGUE

Serving The Tee

In the shadow of segregation, a quiet yet fierce determination surged through San Antonio's Negro community. The Supreme Court's ruling on *Brown v. Board of Education* sent shockwaves across the nation. For Negro golfers of San Antonio, it was a beacon of hope. These athletes, many of whom had lived through the harshest days of segregation, understood that desegregating public golf courses wasn't just about playing a game—it was a fight for dignity and equality.

It was a sweltering Friday night in the third week of June, in San Antonio. The city was gripped by a heatwave spreading across the Midwest, and the air buzzed with heated conversations from news readers and listeners alike. Beneath the cover of night and unghastly heat, a silent battle was brewing. On that Friday evening, June 16, 1954, the San Antonio City Attorney ruled to leave segregation in the hands of the city council. Undeterred, petitioners, driven by an unyielding resolve, had pressed forward, gathering signatures with the intensity of soldiers preparing for war. They knew the stakes were high. The looming terror of lynching hung over them—a grim reminder of the potential consequences of their courageous stand against oppression. The voices of their families echoed in their minds. Some were just one or two generations removed from slavery, with grandparents who had been born free or had survived the horrors of lynching. These petitioners had heard firsthand accounts of their families' histories and the brutal realities of racial violence. Despite the fear, they pressed on.

Brave petitioners, having read the news about the landmark *Brown v. Board Education* ruling, stood in parlors, on porches, in backyards of their neighbors in late May 1954 to quietly gather signatures. While concerned voices hesitated:

"Ey doon wont no lynch mob coming round here."

"Y'all go end up on na *Tree of Sorrow*."

"One aw y'all go end up in da creek."

But youth voices spoke out louder. Some of the young San Antonians drew attention to the nine-year-old caddie from Muny Golf Course in Austin, Texas, whom they had read about in newspapers just four years earlier.

"Look at Alvin Propps. Only nine years old. See how brave he was. People looking like us playing everywhere in Austin."

"And that boy and his friend was arrested too." An elder spoke.

"But look. Them boys wasn't violent. That was how they was protesting, without being violent. We don't want no violence. But we don't wanna follow them Jim Crow laws either."

"Besides, the city council in Austin even suggested all golf courses be open to everybody. Everybody means us too."

"They ain't write no laws lettin' errbody play on they golf parks. They just gave permission for Muny golfing. Just Muny."

But determined voices of those who signed the petition spoke with courage and resolve:

"It ain't just gonna be for Muny. We should be able to play at all the golf courses."

"Our time for equality is now."

"We won't be silenced."

"We deserve to be educated, have our children play, and go places to eat, drink and stand, with dignity like errone else. And not just at the one or two places they say we can."

Their courage, their defiance, would echo far beyond the golf courses of San Antonio, ringing out as a clarion call for equality across the United States. The group had gathered ninety-seven signatures for their petition and sent it via U.S. Postal Service to Ralph Winton, the city manager.

While the petitioners were the vessels of their time, divinely entrusted with the seeds of future generations bestowed by God in that moment, they also became a spark—lighting fairways for future tee time adventures and adventurers.

The ink was still wet on nearly every newspaper in America, despite a historic Midwest heatwave, following the landmark *Brown v. Board of Education* decision. Amid this, the petitioners submitted their compelling petition. While the extreme heat dominated many conversations, it was not a topic of discussion at the San Antonio City Council meeting on Saturday, June 17, 1954, when Mr. Gonzalez read a resolution. With permission, Mr. Gonzalez began with the words: "An ordinance creating a commission for community interrelations." The council went on to appoint members representing a "cross-section of the community." The resolution stated its purpose as a "memorial to citizens and interested officials."[15]

The resolution read by Mr. Gonzalez included these words: "Now, therefore, be it resolved: 1. That all municipally owned and operated golf courses be opened completely, without any restrictions to any user because of color, creed, or racial extraction, to the full use and enjoyment of all citizens.[2] It is further resolved that we disapprove of discrimination against any American." This resolution was read, passed and approved on Thursday June 17, 1954.[15]

By Monday, June 21, the place to celebrate was on the golf course. Not only because it was the traditional day when many golf courses allowed Negros to play, but because for the first time, Negros were permitted to play on any city municipal golf course, on any day the course was open. While twelve Negro golfers chose to play at Willow Springs Golf Course, Mr. Jesse Satterfield and Sgt. Edward Green decided to make history at Brackenridge Golf Course.[16, 17] The pair selected Brackenridge to make history and very well did. Several Newspapers published the story a week later. The San Antonio Register headlined the historic news under the article "Links, Tennis Courts Opened, Pools Closed to Negros." While at the time Negros won the battle for golf desegregation at municipal golf courses, the battle for swimming pools continued the Jim Crow laws of segregation.[17]

That same day Jesse Satterfield and Green broke history, television and newspaper reporters, dressed in three-piece suits, ties, and even bow ties and sweaters despite the heat, gathered at Brackenridge Golf Course. Ladies mostly wore dresses. Regardless of the temperature, a well-dressed crowd of journalists gathered to report, interview, and capture the historic event. While some African Americans played at Willow Springs, two African American men—Mr. Satterfield and Sgt. Green—broke the color line at Brackenridge, a historic course known as the oldest 18-hole golf course in Texas and home to the Texas Golf Hall of Fame. No African Americans had played there before.[16]

Newspaper cameras captured photos of both men donned in tams, Sgt. Edward Green in a white shirt, and Mr. Jesse Satterfield, an employee of Willow Springs Golf Course, in an octagon-patterned collared shirt and slacks. Reporters noted that the men teed off before noon at the historic Brackenridge Golf Course. [16, 17]

By the end of the day, the historic seeds of golf desegregation at municipal golf courses were planted and firmly rooted, ignited by the spark that set ablaze a path for future tee time tales and fairway adventures for future generations to come.

ROUND ONE

Subtle Dynamics

~90 years—four generations later.

T he loud, high-pitch sound of a code blue shattered staff in the intensive care unit at a local teaching hospital in West Los Angeles. The blaring sound of "Code Blue" echoed through the halls, jolting the midnight nursing and resident physician staff out of their routines. Moments before, they had been casually mingling—some glazed at computer stations with coffee cups discreetly hidden between monitors, others chatting by water coolers, hovering over microwaves in the staff lounge, or relaxing with legs propped on empty chairs.

But now, the insistent beeping of the alarm demanded their immediate attention. The ICU staff's collective gaze shifted toward room 1536. For the 3rd time in as many hours, the piercing alarm joined the dull, mechanical voice on the intercom: "Code Blue, room 1536. Code Blue, room 1536." The call rang out again and again, an urgent summons that shattered the veneer of normalcy and propelled the medical team into action.

A crash cart—a typically red, steel mobile cart containing lifesaving medical treatment—was already in the room, restocked and ready to go. Duane, who moments before appeared near lifeless in the intensive care unit, now jerked his body back and forth—violently shaking the bed and equipment in a muscular rage. The doctors initially characterized it as convulsions, but the neurologist has now disputed. There was still no known cause, and doctors had not diagnosed his condition.

Duane miraculously survived a near fatal car crash. His Dodge Chrysler had been totaled and he survived the crash with only minor injuries. All other traumatic head injuries or conditions had been ruled out—eliminated, and now Duane's constant convulsions were beginning to irritate practically all the staff to no end. The neurologist who specialized in seizures evaluated Duane earlier and insisted Duane was not having *seizures* and thus would not diagnose Duane with epilepsy.

"He's just apparently under a lot of stress. He's angry. His actions are not involuntary. He is intentionally shaking his body in a fit of rage," the neurologist said to staff earlier.

"But we can't ignore this," the nursing supervisor explained. "Every time this so-called fit of rage happens, my nurses have to respond, or we'll be liable."

"I'm not advising you to not respond," Dr. Sett instructed. "I'm just disagreeing with administering strong sedatives or anti-convulsant. I carefully looked at and reviewed Dr. Moon's consult report. He's our best psychiatrist on staff. Quite frankly, in Southern California, and I agree. Over medicating this young man would not only delay his recovery, but it could also be detrimental and create unwarranted problems," Dr. Sett said sternly.

The director of nursing was a rotund, formidable European woman with a permanent scowl etched on her face. Her chin was peppered with a few stubborn tufts of fuzz that added to her stern, battel-axe demeanor. She had worked at the hospital for decades, becoming a fixture of unwavering authority and gruffness.

"What would you have us do then?" she barked, her voice grating like gravel. "I don't have staff coverage to keep him at this level of care, especially if we're not medically treating him! He needs to be discharged from our unit and sent to a lower level of care!"

Her tone left no room for negotiation, reflecting years of stubbornness and the ironclad confidence of someone who had argued and fought her way through countless hospital bureaucracies. Earlier, she had clashed with Dr. Stett on every point, but despite her bluster and intimidation, she had lost. Now, she was making one last stand, her posture rigid and her eyes daring anyone to defy her.

"Duane, Duane, Duane," a resident physician assigned to monitor Duane shouted with authority. Her voice, though loud and firm, carried a sweet, savory tone—this time prompting Duane to open his eyes.

Dr. Yazi placed an ungloved hand on Duane's hand as he clasped the physician's fingers. His natural rich milk chocolate complexion was nearly pale moments earlier, hidden and overshadowed by tubes with oxygen in his nose, wires connected to monitoring equipment and IV lines in his left arm. His eyes slowly began to tear.

"Everything's ok Duane. Relax, everything's ok."

"Get this up off me! Let me outta here! Somebody needa come get these damn IVs and this tube outta my nose, before I do!" He proceeded to snatch the tube away from his nose. "Matter'a fact, I know what I'm doin'. Man, move!" He demanded.

"Ok, ok. Nancy, please D/C his IV and O2 stat. I'll certainly hear it from my chief, but let's get you outta the intensive care unit to start."

Duane shook his head in agreement.

"Now you can't go home right away. Dr. Sett and Dr. Moon still want to monitor you before you're discharged. You'll go to a regular room first thing in the morning and they'll see you when they round tomorrow afternoon. Ok?"

"Thank you!"

"But I need you to promise me you'll stop shaking your bed like this. You're making things worse, and we have to make sure you're not having a seizure."

"I'm not have no damn seizure, doctor."

"I know but given your terrible accident and seeing what the car looked like, we can't help but be concerned. It's a wonder you didn't kill yourself."

Duane was transferred out of the ICU. He had only been on the regular floor of the hospital for barely 24 hours when word spread like wildfire across Los Angeles that he was out of the ICU and now able to have visitors. Better known as "Mr. Goodbar" on Instagram, Duane's presence attracted attention far and wide, fans and haters alike.

"Mr. Goodbar," they called him with hint of sexual flavor.

"Who is Mr. Goodbar?" nurse Brianna asked, raising an eyebrow as several ladies approached the nurses' station, eager to visit him. "We don't have anyone by that name," she added, maintaining her professional demeanor.

"Oh," snapping her fingers, "Duane! He's in room 5209."

"Where's room 5209?" asked the shorter of the two young women. They both looked to be about 23 years old, dressed in cut-off jean shorts that barely covered their butt cheeks. The legs of their jean shorts were cut off with rough, jagged edges, the frayed hems hanging with loose threads that gave them a rugged but carefree, worn-out vibe. Both had on matching cropped hoodies. Their designer bags dangled from their elbows, their palms upwards in a perpetually 'selfie-ready' pose.

Brianna, a very tall and attractive Black nurse, new to her position but already competent and confident, was not amused by their antics. However, she couldn't resist probing a bit further.

"Why do they call him Mr. Goodbar?" she asked devilishly, her voice laced with curious skepticism as she briefly escorted the girls towards room 5209.

The girls exchanged knowing glances and simultaneously pursed their lips in an exaggerated manner, clearly drooling with flirtation. Brianna tilted her head, as if a light bulb had just flickered on.

"Um, never mind, I don't think I wanna know." Her voice dropped a few octaves. When she returned to the nurses' station, her coworker LaTanya pulled her aside, whispering discreetly.

"Girl," she began, her voice low but animated. "You ain't never heard of Mr. Goodbar? I never knew his real name, but I've seen him perform before."

"Duane? That patient in 5209, Duane?" Brianna asked, her eyes widening with recognition. "Oh, I think I've seen him on my TL… or maybe the explore page. Guess, I didn't recognize him without the photoshop or one of his vulgar poses," she laughingly admits.

"Yeah, room 5209. That's who's in 5209, the 23-year-old car accident, right?"

Brianna nodded. "He is cute, though."

"Not just cute, girl, that boy is fine! I saw a video of him once…"

Brianna cut LaTanya off. "Girl, please. Don't get in no trouble now," finally understanding the commotion. "Wow, I had no idea. I thought he was just another…regular Black guy."

"I mean, you right about the Black part, but he's definitely poppin'." LaTanya said with a knowing smile. "He has a crazy big following, always hosting parties, getting booked months in advance. He's kind of a big deal. I bet those girls visiting him are probably models or influencers. One of them could be his agent."

"Shut up!" Brianna chuckled, shaking her head. "Guess, I'll have to brush up on my social media to keep up with these young *stars*." She said with air quotes.

"Yes, girl, I'm starting to think you live under a rock. He transferred from ICU, right?"

"Yup, that's why my morning has been so busy. I had a discharge too. I was hoping I'd get him later in the morning, but that's probably why transportation was in a hurry to bring him over. They probably wanted to be the one to transport him before the end of their shift."

"Pretty much. But now I really get the hype about that boy."

"I don't get it. He is 23-years-old fool. That ain't no boy. That's a grown-ass man!"

"You right, but at least he's legal with it."

"What? What are you talking about?"

"Damn, you seriously don't know? He's a stripper…well, exotic dancer, if you wanna be PC. But that body is the hype, girl. I heard he goes out to Venice Beach to compete from time to time, too."

"Competed for what?"

LaTanya rolls her eyes, getting impatient with Brianna being so out the loop, and answered sharply.

"Body building. Didn't you see his arms? I don't know how anyone got an IV in. His skin is so tight, and muscular, and oh we! Nancy mentioned she was the one to get his line in last night."

"Ok, wait. You talked to Nancy about him?"

"Let's just say, the girls that get it, get it."

Brianna rolled her eyes, checking the clock. As a registered nurse she typically stayed on top of her work, but now she was seeing she'd maybe been working a little too much and getting out of touch with things, even with her friends.

"Ok, LaTanya. So, where does he perform?"

"Mostly private parties, like showers. And he's not posting nothing from those. Come to think of it, he barely posts himself, outside of a vanity pic here and there.

"Then how does he get gigs?"

"Word of mouth, of course. I mean, just look at him. But the things other people post of him always go viral and end up on blogs too. I'm sure that's how his account blew up…but none of them are from *him* posting."

"Wow, this is a lot," Brianna laughs.

"Girl, I'm putting you on. I'd show you some of the footage but it's definitely NSFW. I'm not trying to get in trouble here. But obviously the boy's hung."

"Shut up! What?"

"You didn't look?"

"It's not like I needed to put in a foley or something. He's probably 'bout to get discharged outta here cause we ain't doing nothing for him but monitoring him."

"Good thing you got him. I'd probably get in trouble if I had him."

"Girl, shut up."

"Girl, I'm just gettin' started."

The two nurses shared a laugh, marveling at how Duane, or "Mr. Goodbar," had managed to turn a hospital stay into an *Entertainment Tonight* special.

Duane's room was already occupied by a number of visitors, ladies from young to middle-aged. Before long, music was playing in the room, more people showed up carrying balloons, flowers, teddy bears and gift bags.

But Duane received his guests and compliments quite modestly for the nickname of 'Mr. Goodbar.' He adopted the name while in his first year at the state university, still yet a teenager. The name caught on quickly, and 'Mr. Goodbar' became his stage name for several intriguing reasons, some of which were whispered about with affectionate rumors. Although he played football at Cal State U as a defensive back, he also made time and money as a professional male exotic dancer, just short of porn.

When Duane explained to his parents, he started the practice because he needed to raise money to pay his tuition and dorm fees, naturally his parents had many memorable conversations.

But Duane pointed out "y'all are really trippin'. Now I'm wrong for payin' my own way? I'm not doin' drugs, not stealin, not doin' nothin' illegal. Y'all would let me tear up my body in football, but I can't get some money off how good it look?"

"I know how I raised you son." His mom said emphatically. "I did…"

"You?" his father, more liberal-minded interrupted saying.

"We," turning to her husband. The middle-aged Black couple still lived together in their modest home, in a historic district near View Park, California. "We didn't raise a criminal or a drug addict. *We*, raised you to be a responsible young man Duane. *We* taught you how to respect not only other people, but yourself too. *We* taught you to not misuse what God gave you, son. You know better." His mom, Mae said in one breadth.

"Well...he is a Black man, babe. My son is well-endowed like his ole man," slapping Duane on the back and grabbing his shoulder. "God didn't have any shortage when he passed out our..."

"Shut up James! I don't want ma son getting in no trouble over some girl accusing him wrongly. Long as he respects women and knows NO means NO." She turned to Duane and said, "I want you to remember son, when a woman says 'no' that means no. Never force yourself on to anyone for anything, you hear me?!"

Duane looked slowly nodding his head in a gesture of 'yes' to his mother and shaking his head in frustration towards his dad.

"All I gotta say is, boy, protect yourself, son. When you doin' yo thang you gotta check some of these so-called girls. For one, you don't know what they got. It may look good, but you get in them panties it ain't what you think it is. Believe dat!" Imitating Tupac's voice. "You could come out with something you didn't take in! And if it don't smell good, it ain't good."

Duane grinned sideways towards his dad. His mother didn't see neither fella's smirk. Despite Duane's parents' difference and emphasis on rearing philosophy, Duane listened to both and took to heart every word said.

However, there was one thing both parents agreed on: "If you go out making babies remember, it's your responsibility to take care it. Don't have any 'til you can take care of 'em. Every last one!" Both of his parents were dedicated to teaching him how to grow up and be a 'respectful young man.'

But even before his nickname, Duane's mother emphasized at an early age: "Be conscientious, son. You can't always wear what you see some of these other young men wearing. You gotta look in the mirror and make sure you're not advertising. If a young lady's gonna be attracted to you, it should be for your character and not your penis!"

"He ain't gotta be ashamed of it, Mae. But son," turning sternly toward Duane, "I don't ever wanna see you walking around wit cho pants saggin'. Ain't no body gonna hire you showing yo draws. And a mothafucka wit they pants down is a invitation to get poked in da ass."

"James!"

"Hey Mae, I'm tellin' you what I know goes on when a brotha' gets locked up. Dat shit means they wanna get it in da…"

"Shut up, James."

Duane's dad tried to hide gesturing a flip of his middle finger pointing towards his rear end, but Mae caught it from the side of her eye. James was a very tall, dark mahogany salt and pepper Black man with a rugged beard, short haircut and numerous old cut marks on his face from fighting at a young age, getting the street education that enriched him when he became an adult. Mae shook her head in disgust.

"And you sho' can't run fast if yo pants hanging down, can you?"

"Sometime a brotha gotta get down da road and handle they business," Mr. James topped off walking out of the room. Duane snickered at both his parent's innuendos.

Nevertheless, Duane was a social kid his entire life. He'd talk to anyone at any time, carrying both messages from his parents. He made a point to speak with everybody, from his neighbors when they were watering their yard, to complete strangers in the grocery store shopping, people at the mall, church, wherever and whenever and regardless of age or race. He had no hesitation to approach strangers, or even the unapproachable. In Duane's junior year of high school, he was the homecoming prince, and in his senior year prom king. He played football and basketball, humbly sporting his letterman jacket with blue jeans on the daily.

Duane won on and off the field, naturally. All the girls loved him—with or without a letterman jacket on. But one in particular, Genie—a diligent student, who stayed focused on her studies and enjoyed theatre—was unimpressed by Duane and his popular crowd. When he invited Genie to the prom, she had just finished a performance in her theatre class. She declined Duane's invitation, along with invitations from several other guys. Genie had already decided not to go to the prom, even before any of the guys invited her.

"He's way too cocky for me," Genie told a friend. When Duane heard about her comment, he thought he could win her over by asking her to the prom and waited for just the right moment. But Genie, in her forthright manner, replied to Duane, "No, thank you." She also told her friend. "I also told him I thought he was overly opinionated, dismissive, and too talkative," she added.

"Girl, what did he say?"

"He just said thank you and walked away."

Duane, remembering his upbringing that 'no means no,' had gone out of his way by attending Genie's theatre class to ask her, but after she turned him down, he moved on without further debate.

By 23 years of age, Duane's life took a tragic turn with a severe car crash. Just before his discharge from the hospital, he was visited by a police officer, a resident physician, and a forensic intern. The passenger in the other car had died, and the district attorney was considering charging Duane with murder.

"Murder! But that car ran the light and hit me!" Duane protested. The police officer explained that all evidence needed to be considered, and an investigation of the car crash had commenced. What worried Duane most was the forensic intern—it was Genie, his old classmate. He feared she might be biased against him.

The events of that year would shape Duane's entire life. On the same day he was discharged from the hospital, his father suffered a heart attack and died upon hearing his only son could be charged with murder. Without the extra money from his dance shows and body building contests, Duane struggled to pay tuition while also covering funeral expenses for his dad. Adding to his burden, his only sister moved back home after getting pregnant, leaving Duane to support his mother, sister, and newborn niece.

Determined to turn his life around, Duane landed a job with a real estate investor. His social skills and life's hard lessons became his bread and butter, eventually creating a new stream of wealth. Despite his earlier challenges, Duane transformed his life through resilience and perseverance.

By the time Genie saw Duane again years later, he was a different man, with a new career to match. He was perched at the white marble bar, settled comfortably on a sleek barstool. The stool's white cushions elegantly accented the marble, while the column and sling back gleamed in a sophisticated gold, reflecting the upscale ambiance of the popular LA bar. Duane was deep in an intense conversation with Genie's boyfriend, Alan.

"Wow, so a negative toxicology report was likely the best piece of evidence the DA used to clear you of murder?" Alan insisted, his tone probing.

"No, man, not just that," Duane responded, his voice rising. "There were security cameras, witnesses, and everything. There was nothing except lies from the other driver. I shouldn't have even been charged in the first place!" He was growing increasingly irritated with Alan's insistence.

Unbeknownst to Duane, Alan was an attorney and enjoyed debating such matters. Alan had also made numerous references about his girlfriend, Genie, completing an internship as a forensic analyst. But Alan represented to Duane that Genie—not stating her name, was his fiancé. This constant emphasis was starting to annoy Duane, especially since Alan, a White man, continued to defend the district attorney's wrongful suspicions.

"No disrespect, man," Duane continued, his patience wearing thin, "but I'm tellin' you what I know, not what someone else thinks they know. I was there, not your fiancée. I don't care who she works for. I was there, not you or her. The police should never have even considered a murder charge."

At that moment, Genie walked up, catching the tail end of the heated exchange. She paused at the door, her heart skipping a beat when she recognized Duane and both men's body language. She felt her throat tightening and began to breathe rapidly. Instead of walking over to greet Alan and Duane, Genie ducked into the bathroom to gather herself, but her breathing became more and more irregular. She stepped into one of the stalls, put the seat cover down and sat still for a moment to catch her breath.

Why is he here? She thought and sat looking up at the ceiling fanning herself with her hand. After several moments of composure, she stepped out of the stall, washed her hands, and dabbed a little cool water on her face. She checked her hair and lipstick, took a few deep breaths, and tried to evaluate her feelings. Seeing Duane again stirred up a lot of emotions. Genie wasn't quite sure how to face the music and was nervous.

Finally composed, Genie made her way over to the bar, briefly glancing at her reflection in the glass and mirror tile ceiling. The tension was palpable as she approached the men. Duane's eyes flicked to her, a mix of surprise and something else she couldn't quite read. "Oh, my god," she said underneath her breath feeling her lips move and suspecting Duane could read her lips' motion.

"Hey, Genie," Alan greeted her with a forced cheerfulness and kiss on her lips. He pulled Genie close to him. "This is Duane. Duane, this is Genie, my," he hesitated and added "fiancée."

Genie's neck slowly turned her face forced a smile, before looking sternly at Alan. Her eyes betraying a flicker of anger at Alan, and recognition. Duane keenly observing the couple's unsubtle interaction.

"Hi, Duane. It's been minute." Eyes widened.

Duane nodded; his expression guarded. "Yup, yup. Wassup Genie?"

Alan, oblivious to the undercurrent, lacking insight on how to respond, "Duane, here, was just telling me about his experience with the district attorney. Quite the story, huh?"

Genie made a muffled 'oomph' sound, barely parting her lips, the noise escaping from the back of her throat like a stifled exclamation, then said while grimacing, "I remember hearing about it."

Duane could see the awkwardness in her demeanor and the tension in her posture. He couldn't resist probing a little.

"So, Genie, congratulations are in order." He glanced at her left ring finger and continued: "Still working in forensics?"

Alan reached and grabbed Genie's left hand and kissed it. Genie looked at Alan curiously and with disagreement.

Alan interrupted her before she could answer.

"We're not officially engaged," pausing while seeking Genie's nonverbal approval, "but she is the woman I want to marry," placing emphasis on 'is.'

Genie clenched her teeth and ignored Alan's statement while slowly sliding her hand out of Alan's and directed her reply to Duane.

"Yes, I am," she said, a little too quickly. "It's challenging but rewarding."

"Challenging, huh?" Duane's eyes locked onto hers. "I bet you seen a lot."

Genie shifted uncomfortably, sensing the intensity in Duane's gaze. Her lips began to quiver.

"Yes, I've had my share."

Alan, sensing the tension but misunderstanding its source, tried to lighten the mood.

"Genie's always been the best at what she does. I'm lucky to have her."

Duane raised an eyebrow, detecting the subtle unease between the couple.

"Yeah man, I'm happy to see it."

Alan smiled, missing the subtle edge in Duane's tone

"Absolutely. She's amazing."

Genie blushed, looking down and away then again at her reflection behind the bar.

"Thanks, Alan."

Duane couldn't shake the feeling that there was more to Genie's reaction than just professional pride. He decided to test the waters further. "So, Genie, what's been good? Any interesting cases, lately?"

She looked up, her eyes meeting his briefly in the ceiling's reflection before darting away, then back into his face.

"Oh, you know, the usual. Nothing as dramatic as your case, though."

"Right," Duane said slowly, leaning back on the barstool and folding his arms while one foot on footrest. He swiveled back and forth on the barstool and said, "nothing as dramatic, huh?"

"Wait, excuse me. Have you two met before?"

While Genie struggled for an explanation, Duane decided to add more mischief.

"This amazing woman once turned me down for the prom in high school." Duane's subtle smirk revealed a tiny dimple in his left cheek.

"Babe, I thought you didn't go to your prom."

"I didn't. I didn't go with anyone. I just didn't want to go."

"Relax, man, she was obviously waiting for you." Duane said standing up and rubbing his hands through is short curly hair. His muscular six-foot-three statue was somewhat softened since Genie last saw him when he was at the height of his body building and dancing. Duane stood with his shoulder squared off and looked Genie directly into her eyes. Genie, aware of Duane's nickname, couldn't resist taking a quick glance below Duane's belt. She was slow to look away and Alan noticed her eye's shifting and stood to his feet.

Alan, though not nearly as tall as Duane, stood several inches shorter in stature. Even so, he still edged out Genie in height, despite the four-inch boost from her stilettos that complemented her lean, curvaceous five-foot frame. Duane's muscular build further emphasized the contrast between the two men, making Alan's presence seem modest by comparison.

Alan adjusted his posture, straightening his shoulders to add a touch more height while subtly drawing attention to his well-tailored suit. He was an attractive, slender white man with a peachy complexion, his dirty blond hair neatly cropped, and his face clean-shaven. Often, his fingers would find their way to his dimpled chin and sideburns, a habitual gesture that hinted at his self-awareness.

"Hey," extending his hand to Duane, "why not join us for dinner. I'd love to hear more about you and Genie's high school days."

Duane paused and waited for Genie to respond. But she was flat and avoided eye contact with both men. His keen observation skills picked up on the subtle dynamics between Genie and Alan. While Alan seemed genuinely proud of Genie, there was an undercurrent of discomfort that he couldn't quite place.

"Thanks. It's cool, I don't wanna impose. We can all catch up another time," Duane finally answered saying. Genie looked into Duane's eyes with disappointment, but Duane felt she was relieved. Despite her attempts to hide her feeling, Duane could see the attraction she had towards him and that she was trying hard to mask and deny. And while he respected her relationship with Alan, he couldn't help but wonder why the couple appeared distant from one another.

"Good meeting you, Alan," extending his hand.

"You too… *Bro.*" Duane was ready to walk away despite catching Alan's tone when he said 'Bro,' but Alan made the mistake of taking the conversation one step too far. As if testing Duane.

"Maybe we can shoot some *hoop*?"

But there was something about the emphasis Alan put on *bro*, and *hoop* that sounded unnatural and forced, which triggered Duane. Alan hadn't seemed congenial through their entire conversation, and Duane never mentioned anything about basketball. He looked at Genie for her response, and her brow was sternly raised at Alan. Instinctively she challenged him, hoping to preempt a snappy response from Duane.

"Since when do you play basketball, *babe*," tilting her head emphasizing *babe*.

Although Alan was exposed, Duane respected Genie and pivoted.

"I'm gonna have to decline, I gave up basketball a while ago. But, if you got a good swing and ever down for hitting the links, I'm all for a round of golf, instead," then winked at Genie before walking away.

As Duane left, he couldn't help but glance back one last time. He caught Genie watching his every move. Though her face had a little smirk, her eyes were filled with a mixture of regret and longing. It was a look that stayed with Duane long after he left the bar.

Reception Ballad

Securely embraced by my groom's arms,
Our first dance after saying, "I do"
Visions of paradise kept time for our feet
As we dance sweet harmony, and twirled to the beat,
Our guests behold beauty their memory will keep

My ultimate love, I vowed to you at the alter
In exchange for the vows, you gave me
Wrapped in your eyes, that penetrate my heart,
I pray no tomorrows of us ever apart

Ah! That man that gazes there beyond the threshold of our
reception
Yes, I knew him for some time
With round shoulders, he once embraced these curves,
That memory once escapes me is happily blurred.
There were days we sang our alma mater,
When you carried another's books every day
You promised each other a future in life
But it is I, now your loving wife
Dancing with you
As the music softly plays
Comparing our past from today

Now I dance before two men
Reflecting till the music ends

As the tempo pick up, as the bows swiftly swing,
Violins, beat the ivory, and orchestra strings!
I'm closing my eyes to make sure of the beat,
Drifting in fantasy, some say feeding conceit,
But now I awaken from a nightmarish dose,
Returning the past to mere threshold view,
Gazing through the door of our reception.

I open my eyes,
In real time I see
The man whom I vowed,
Dancing in harmony.

Garden Hole

*S*everal years later, Duane, twenty-six, and Genie, twenty-five, had been married for a little less than two years. The two were happily married without children, still learning about one another just eight years out of high school. Genie completed her internship and landed a great job with the county as a forensic DNA analyst. A forensic DNA analyst is a detective who uses special tools to study tiny bits of the body called DNA. DNA is like a code that makes all living organisms unique. DNA is like a secret password.

As a forensic analyst, Genie's job was to collect DNA from crime scenes or people suspicious for committing a crime and compares it to other samples to see if the DNA matched. She was also assigned the duty to write reports and go to court to tell what she found. Like detectives, Genie's work helps catch criminals and solve mysteries using the special code of DNA. Genie's job as a DNA analyst sometimes required her to also testify in court as an expert witness to explain her findings. Essentially, she used her expertise as a science major to uncover the truth behind crimes.

By then, only on a few occasions had Genie crossed paths with Alan. At no time did she have regrets. However, Alan always seemed embarrassed when she saw him. Genie had learned Alan was a big fake not long after running into Duane that night at the bar when she was with Alan. A chance encounter with Duane while she was in court downtown solidified her suspicions.

"Did you and Alan finally tie the knot?" At that time Duane asked Genie casually, recalling Alan's false claim and the uncomfortable glance Genie had given Alan that night at the bar.

Genie shook her head and turned up her lip.

"We were never engaged."

Duane nodded in agreement—as if he already knew. He exposed a hint of relief through his eyes.

"Well, watch yourself. He's an attorney, right?"

Genie rolled her eyes, "a personal *injury* attorney at that."

"Oh, I see," Duane chuckled. "And you work with a lot of police and detectives? I could see him trying to poach some clients off you; I wouldn't trust him."

Duane caught Genie's subtle interest and longing for him during that brief encounter. The shared history of his car crash investigation during his hospitalization, combined with his genuine concern for her safety, created a bond between them. Duane didn't hesitate to invite Genie to exchange contact information, and she didn't resist.

One text message turned into many nights of deep conversations, followed by an invitation to meet up again. Soon, a series of dates unfolded, and they both surrendered to the undeniable chemistry between them, drawn together by a magnetic pull they couldn't resist. Beyond the heat of desire, the couple also shared a deep mutual respect and affection for one another. They especially enjoyed walks along nearby streams and barefoot in the sand at the beach. Neither could resist dancing together at backyard pool parties and going to jazz festivals together. Every date deepened their connection and blossomed into profound love that culminated in a short engagement and ultimately a beautiful marriage.

They purchased a single-story home nestled in a tree-lined street. The magical city of Willow Springs sat just outside the bustling city of Irvine in Orange County, California. A sun-soaked, family-friendly community with unique boutiques and charming dining spots, it was an enchanting blend of suburban tranquility and coastal charm. They both enjoyed Orange Country's dry dusky breeze and evening cool breeze of the blue sea.

Soon after moving, Genie convinced Duane to get a Rottweiler puppy which she named Sir Duke. Duke was a young Rottweiler true to his breed. He was very smart, loyal and protective. Moreover, however, Duke had a keen sense of awareness—a very powerful "spatial" awareness.

Spatial awareness is like having a GPS map inside the brain. There are two areas in the brain that controls spatial awareness. Both are near the bottom: the cerebellum and the brainstem. Humans and most Animals have spatial awareness. Spatial awareness is one of six body's senses which include taste, vision, hearing, smell, touch and a sense called proprioception. The spatial awareness helps interactions with the world around. It helps humans and animals know their body's position in relation to the earth.

To know one's environment in time and space, one needs to be aware of the size, shape, and location of objects in physical space, as well as the ability to navigate and move within that space effectively. Duke's spatial awareness was one of his best senses after the sense of smell, which is dog's best sense. Duke's keen sense of awareness made him the most alert canine around. He was perfect to serve as

Duane's service animal, Genie insisted on Duane having after his first scary allergy attack.

A service dog is not just for comfort or emotional support. A service dog is one that is trained to perform special duties for the owner. By now, Duane had been playing play golf for years. He had given up basketball at the advice of his friend and mentor Glen. Glen had become a key person in Duane's life following the accident and all the stress he endured surrounding the investigation which caused his father's fatal heart attack. Glen was a local teen coach, older family man and retired trial attorney. Duane had known Glen for years prior but during Duane's turmoil, he turned to Glen for advice and mentorship. As a confidant, he also mentioned to Glen about his encounter with Alan and Genie. Glen was able to verify Duane's suspicion which in turn, Duane was able to give Genie the pivotal head's up which changed the young trio's lives' forever.

Unlike basketball—a high impact sport, golf doesn't require running or jumping which puts a lot of stress on the knees and ankles. Golf is a low impact sport. As a low impact sport, golfers spend more time on a padded grass surface. This helps players avoid many stress-related injuries that can occur on hard surfaces like concrete and wood. Many people enjoy golfing and feel golfing is a fun sport. Since practically all ages can play golf, many people find it not only relaxing but also a great way to meet people from all walks of life.

Several months after the couple were married Duane suddenly experienced severe allergic reactions. For a long time, doctors couldn't figure out what was causing Duane's allergies. Especially since Duane's job as a real estate investor was mostly indoors. His love for golf wouldn't allow him to give up the sport, though, especially since the game helped Duane handle stress. But Genie convinced Duane to get a service dog because dogs have a keen sense of smell. Genie selected Duke after recognizing Duke had a heightened awareness. Genie studied puppy videos every day before the puppy was weened and had a sense of his behavior before they even got him.

Genie spent a lot of time researching and investigating possible allergens that caused Duane's allergic reactions. It was Genie's investigative work that she learned in her field that pointed to the cause of Duane's severe allergic reactions, specific bird feathers. She began explaining to Duane that Duke's keen spatial awareness would allow Duke to identify the presence of these specific birds' feathers so Duane could avoid ever even encountering them. Additionally, she pointed out, Duke could have Duane's medication readily available if he passed out from an allergic reaction. Duane not only loved Genie, but he also trusted her professional opinion, especially since Genie was on the forensic team that help clear him of any wrong doing and avoid any wrongful criminal charge.

While birds could be found almost everywhere, doctors recently learned Duane would only have an allergic reaction to certain species of a few birds who managed to have the mite in its wings. Only close contact with those specific birds that had the wing mites posed a threat to Duane's health, causing the allergic reaction. Even though it was a very small chance he would encounter a bird that had the insect mites, a very bad reaction could threaten Duane's life if he didn't get medical attention in time.

Genie continued explaining to Duane that an allergic reaction occurs when the body overreacts to something. The overreaction, or allergic reaction, usually occurs when body (the immune system) becomes confused and believes the body must protect itself (by using soldiers) from some sort of invasion of harmless things.

"Usually," Genie went on to explain, "these harmless things are plant particles, food, dust, sometimes animal fur or even grass," she said. "The immune system starts sending soldiers out to fight. The process of fighting is called a defense. It's like the body is needlessly fighting something harmless."

She went on to correctly tell Duane that if the reaction were very mild, he would only require an antihistamine in the form of a capsule.

"But if the reaction is severe, honey, you'll need an injection."

"An injection?!"

"Yes babe, a shot. The shot contains adrenalin also known as a medicine called epinephrine. It makes the heart pump faster to speed up your body's fighting response." She explained to Duane that he could carry both medications in an emergency bag which would be carried around the dog's neck.

"Look, I'll just wear a medical bracelet and be done." Duane tried to appeal to Genie without completely dismissing her suggestion. Whenever matters concerned medical issues, Duane always deferred to Genie. "Babe, one of my friends' wife is a nurse. She said I could simply wear a medical bracelet on my wrist." Duane always preferred simplicity. A medical bracelet is frequently worn by many people who have medical diagnosis requiring immediate attention by first responders. The bracelet alerts medical personnel at first sight of the person's need, prior to initiating treatment. It's a warning before treatment starts. Paramedics and other medical providers look for medical bracelets or medical necklace tags as an initial warning. The tags have a summary of the person's need without having to access a person's telephone if that person is alone and unable to speak for themselves.

After a little coercion, Duane went along with Genie's recommendation, more so to please his wife. He and Genie purchased Duke as a puppy from a very special breeder in Florida, at Evie's Garden. Evie's Garden was also a buffalo ranch. A harmonious coexistence or perhaps even an ecosystem paradise where bulls and heifers (female cows) were raised for grazing or meat production. Within this enchanting ranch, an extraordinary breed of Rottweilers were professionally bred, raised, and, once old enough, sold to select owners.

Evie Lynn was very selective with the applicants for her puppies. Would-be owners were selected by Mrs. Evie, after an application was carefully reviewed. Once the applicants were selected, they were required to undergo training prior to finalizing their purchase. After Genie and Duane completed their online training, the couple flew from John Wayne Airport in Orange County to Orlando to pick up their puppy.

Duke was trained to not only smell the certain insect mite, but also detect the odor Duane's body produced when he was about to have a reaction. Whenever Duane was in danger of encountering a dangerous feather containing the mite nearby, Duke would know immediately because Duke was able to smell it. Once Duke would detect the mite, he would communicate to Duane by tapping his chest moments before the reaction would become dangerous. By knowing a reaction were afoot, sooner than later, Duane would have more time to take one the medications stored in the medical bag Duke carried around his neck.

Duane and Genie named the medical bag Rover because the name Rover combined the idea of preparedness ("ready") with Duke's role as a loyal companion ("rover"). Also, the name Rover emphasized the functionality of the bag as a compact emergency kit and added a playful touch to the name.

From the moment Genie and Duane picked up Duke from Evie's Garden, they both loved him. However, it took several months for Duke to complete additional training for the job he had to perform, to assist and protect Duane during allergic reactions. Eventually Duke and Duane developed their own special form of communication. While Genie remained skeptical about Duke and Duane's communication, she knew Duke had undergone amazing training to help save Duane if ever a need to. She felt secure because Duke always carried the Rover medical bag around his neck.

The trio had a very special bond, and the couple relied on Duke and trusted Duke's training. Of course, ever so often Duke's remarkable abilities were tested. Take for instance the day at Willow Springs golf course when an alligator not native to California invaded the golf course.

Ode To Summer

A dry dusky breeze
A cool breeze off the blue sea
So warm those days, you hyper sun
As soon as the sun settles, another day has begun.

Sherbet's melting behind the waters
As the sun casts orange flavor glaze
Foam creams the jungle rocks
While the salt returns to waves

I thought I left you on the trail up stream,
in search for cooler grounds.
You met me sliding back down path,
Knowing I'd turn back around.

Summer, you know I love to walk
With my feet exposed and bare
You greeted me at the end of spring
Knowing I'd see you right there

Fascination filled my eyes
But with your heat there's no surprise
As how you creep beneath those cracks,
To pop those bugs like crackerjacks

And yet some eve, some calm, some still
Some moons are known to send a chill
As lovers gaze beneath your light
Some creep, some crawl,
Some only at night.

A dry dusky breeze
A cool breeze off the blue sea
We danced to your rays, cause your heat kept us live,
Our love for life will forever survive.

Sherbet melted behind the waters
As the sun cast orange flavor glaze
Visions of July
Etched rainbow clouds in the sky
For the return of those hot summer days!

ROUND THREE

Tee Time Battle

Genie received a phone call Sunday night, one late spring evening. The couple had come home late after a sunset beach-side Jazz Festival. Genie was informed she needed to be at a briefing early the next morning for a crime scene investigation scheduled to open. It was not unusual for Genie to get an advance about a crime scene because many times police are "investigating subjects" under suspicion of a crime being committed. Once enough evidence has been gathered, police may proceed with obtaining permission from a judge to conduct a deeper investigation of a covert search warrant called a "sneak and peak."

Weeks earlier police had begun to suspect a home in the city was keeping illegal animals for pets, and that some of the pets may have managed to escape. There had been a number of calls from surrounding communities about strange animal and bird noises at a specific house but now a photo of an alligator sighting surfaced.

"When are people going to stop trying to keep wild animals as pets?" Genie was leaving the kitchen when she answered her phone.

"Something similar happened 15 years ago in Harbor City. Some idiot released an alligator." Said Officer Mike.

"Yes, Reggie! I remember that fool. I was a kid at the time."

"Yup, well, I won't date myself," the officer laughed and stated. "But I will tell you we caught those knuckleheads."

"I read. And I believe the alligator is still living at the Los Angeles Zoo."

"That gator may still be here when I'm dead and gone. They can live as long as humans. Some can even reach 100 years old. Anyway, the mayor's arranging a press conference for first thing in the morning. She's planning to alert neighborhoods in the Willow Springs area to watch their small children and pets."

"Hey, that's my area. My husband and I live in Willow Springs!"

"Probably why the Chief put you on the team for this case. She probably wants you to come in to analyze some of the clandestine evidence we've gathered.

"Ok," Genie said proudly. This would be the biggest assignment she's had so far. "I'll be sure to come in a little early for briefing," she replied between sips of water and went down the hall to bed. Duane and Duke had already turned in for the night.

The next morning Duane and Duke had gotten up even before Genie's alarm went off. They were already about to leave the house by the time she woke up.

It was late spring in the city of Willow Springs, a tranquil retreat compared to the bustling beachside neighboring cities. While close enough to be influenced by the commercial beach culture, portions of Willow Springs featured picturesque foothill terrain. Lush, rolling hills with gentle slopes and natural undulations created a scenic and sometimes challenging landscape for homes and roads, exemplifying California's diverse and varied landscape.

Genie and Duane's home was situated in a newly developed community. This area, previously untouched, now boasted modern homes amidst the scenic foothill terrain called Willow Springs, offering a serene escape with the charm of lush, rolling hills and gentle slopes, though not many miles from the beach. Both had slept well. There were no honking horns or bustling traffic. Not even the usual symphony of nature's orchestra—chirping of birds serenaded. Although bird's harmonizing was a pleasant sound for most, it always served as a reminder to Genie, Duane, and Duke of the potential for Duane to have a dangerous reaction. Ever since Duane's first reaction, the threat of another was inescapable. The couple hadn't been married long after the first reaction, and the memory was still fresh.

"You guys up already?" Genie asked Duane while rubbing sleep from her eyes. Duane had walked back into the bedroom to kiss Genie goodbye.

"Morning, baby." Duane whispered while leaning in to kiss his wife, her honey-toned complexion glowing softly. Her athletic, sculpted body lay sprawled across the bed, as carefree as the serene expression on her face. Duane paused to admire her beauty and innocence.

"You were all over the bed last night. You must've been still dancing to the jazz music in your sleep."

"Me! You were the one snoring."

"Welcome to my world."

"Seriously."

Duane leaned in and kissed Genie on the lips.

"We're getting an early tee time ahead of the crowd today. Bill's been talking too much mess lately and I gotta serve him up right."

Genie smiled, then squirmed and stretched her long legs.

"I need to get up too. I got a call late last night for an early briefing."

"Tell dispatch not to call you after ten. Ain't nothing that damn important."

Duane turned and walked out the room, but Genie jumped up.

"You guys be careful!" She quickly glanced up to see the time displayed on their ceiling's projection digital clock. "Duane," she shouted. "Duane! Don't you think it's too early? The sun's not even out now."

Duane turned and walked back into the room, Duke in tow.

"Stop hollering in the next room babe. I can't hear you. Now what were you saying?"

"Well, damn. Why you gotta be so cranky this early?"

"I ain't cranky. I just don't wanna be hollered at. I told you this many times and you keep doing it. Why I gotta be called some 'cranky shit' 'cause I don't want be hollered at?"

"Jeez!" Genie complained out loud. She recognized her husband's edgy nature and shook her head in a moment of disgust and sighed. "I think it's entirely too early for y'all to be at some golf course. Besides…"

Duane didn't let her finish her warning. Genie wanted to let Duane know about the strange investigation assignment but as police policy non-public information on suspected criminality were confidential.

"Baby, I'm a grown ass man. Anybody out there this early might wanna steer clear of two Black men with iron clubs in their hands, if they know what's good fa them!" Duane started walking back out of the bedroom leaving Genie speechless. "Besides, I have a meeting in the office this afternoon. Today's ma day to go in this week. And

Bill's ass is heading to New York for the next couple of weeks. I need to straighten him out a bit."

Duane and his faithful Rottie left the house for Willow Springs golf course. The manager had indeed given them a pre-opening tee time to as a favor for Bill helping him with his stock picks. Duane and Duke pulled slowly out of the garage. The early morning air was crisp and cool, night-blooming jasmine still lingered in the air. Duke rode harnessed by seat belts in the back seat of the car. His keen senses constantly on alert, nose twitching with anticipation. Duane sipped his coffee behind the wheel for their short drive to the golf course.

The men had scheduled for a pre-dawn tee time. A tee time in golf is like a reservation for playing on the golf course. Just like when you make a reservation at a restaurant to ensure you have a table, golfers make tee times to ensure they have a spot to play on the course. It's like saying, 'Okay, at this time, it's our turn to start playing golf!' So, when you have a tee time, you know exactly when you get to start your golf adventure.

Willow Springs golf course was not far from Duane and Genie's home. It sat on the border of two cities and was one of the best kept secrets in town. It was hidden at the bottom of a hillside, not visible by those unfamiliar. The foothills, though not landscaped and full of brush, were a natural beauty given the lakes and streams that formed by the runoff from a main drain. While the small slopes in winter were narrow and perilous, the streams made for great trails in the late fall. However, it was late spring, and the runoff was plentiful this year, given California's high rain the last several seasons.

Willow Springs golf course was an 18-hole course. A golf course is like a big playground for relaxation, socialization, and friendly competition. Imagine a long trail with different spots called 'holes' along the way. Each hole has a special area called a 'tee' where you start, and you must hit the golf ball into a small hole called the 'cup' at the end. After you finish one hole, you move on to the next until you've played 18 holes.

Today the fellas chose Willow Springs because the men knew they'd have a fun and adventure with lots of different challenges to overcome along the way. The course was wide open without a lot of tree lines. Duane especially loved the course because it was close to his home. Duane encouraged his friends to play the course and told them: *'Bro, if you pay attention, you'll play well. I pay attention, so you know how I do.'*

Golf gave the men a little fun and adventure with lots of different challenges to overcome along the way. Duane enjoyed playing golf with Billy-Ray aka Bill aka Billie. The two were high school buddies with different careers but both dealing with money. Duane was still doing well as a real estate investor, and Billy a stockbroker. Neither men nor Genie had yet turned thirty years old.

A stockbroker is someone who helps people buy and sell stocks, which are small pieces of ownership in a company. Imagine you have some money and want to invest it in a company like Apple or Google. You would tell the stockbroker what you want to buy or sell, and they would handle the process for you. They give you advice on what might be a good investment and make sure the transactions happen smoothly. It's a bit like having a coach who knows all about the game of buying and selling parts of companies. Billy-Ray aka Bill frequently traveled to New York for his company.

Willow Springs golf course was the perfect blend of par three, four and five holes. The fairways are lined with a variety of majestic oak and pine trees, several rolling hillsides, and lush green grass, which a local volunteer historic society is dedicated to upkeep. Several picturesque ponds create an endless serene atmosphere locals are proud of.

Duane spotted his friend Bill as soon as he and Duke went into the clubhouse.

"Hey, Duane! You decided to show up for another loss," Bill said exaggerating his chest poked, then had a large grin.

"Man, if ya lucky, you might be able to pick up a few pointers. You betta watch me work!" Returning Bill's smile and swollen chest, and his own sarcastic grin. Duane and many of their friends, including Bill had attended the same high school. But Bill and Duane had been friends since elementary school and always enjoyed playfully teasing each other. Although both were competitive, they always showed good sportsmanship—a lesson both their parents always taught them.

Duke wagged his tail enthusiastically, his dark eyes sparkling with excitement as he took in the familiar sights and smells of the golf course. Meanwhile, the TV in the reception area was tuned to the local news, where a story about an unexpected visitor had captured the attention of the community.

"I'm watching this crazy news report 'bout a kid who was attacked or bit by some sort of wild animal. Get this, the kid is sayin' it was a monkey!"

"A monkey! Now where did that child get close enough to get bit by a damn monkey? The zoo?"

"Nah man, not the zoo. Right here in your own city, man—in Willow Springs. Could be down the street, you betta watch out."

"Aight man, you crazy," Duane said impatiently. "But that ain't gone be no excuse for you today."

JJ the club manager interrupted the men to take their payment before responding.

"Well, maybe the kid just didn't wanna go to…"

"Wait, here comes a press conference," Bill said looking at the TV.

The journalist's reporting was interrupted by a press conference with the mayor. The men were busy changing the subject and teasing one another. Neither of them turned to listen to the rest of the press release.

"It could be real. Remember that alligator spottin' in Harbor City, they named him Reggie. Man, Reggie was famous after that shit."

"I still can't figure out how a fuckin alligator ended up shittin' in a Southern California man-made lake? That still don't make no damn sense. People from everywhere was going to Harbor Park to catch a glimpse of that mothafucka."

"Yeah, man. It's wild. Food trucks going to feed spectators, people buying Tee shirts named 'Reggie' and shit."

"What a time. That's capitalism at its fuckin finest," Bill said.

While the three men chatted, Duke's flat ears moved back behind his head at the mention of an elusive alligator. His senses tingled with curiosity. He stood near Duane looking at the TV screen. But the three men were talking over the press conference.

"I think someone had it as a pet, illegally. It either got out or was brought to the lake after it got too large. Whoever owned it probably couldn't keep it in their home any longer."

"That's sad actually. When are people gonna learn not to keep fuckin wild animals in their home?" Said Bill.

"Yeah, the last time I heard about someone having a monkey as a pet, someone's face got gashed."

"Man, that wasn't a monkey, that was a chimpanzee." Bill said to Duane while grabbing the keys to the golf cart.

"Same thing. Chimp, monkey. Same difference."

"Man, monkeys have tails. Chimps are bigger and smarter, more like humans."

"And probably got a better golf swing than you, too."

The press conference was on TV when the guys left. JJ had turned the TV down while the guys were kidding one another. He always enjoyed hearing the men boast about their swing and tease one another. The two men left the club house to board the two-seat golf cart. Duane navigated the two down the lush green fairways with Duke trotting in front to scare away possible mite carrying birds in their path. His senses were alert and vigilant. With Duke's keen sense of smell and spatial awareness, Genie—at home—felt safer than ever, knowing Duke would always be nearby to alert Duane of any potential danger and give him the emergency bag. However, Duane only went along with the idea to appease Genie.

Nevertheless, Duke always carried the emergency bag on his neck with his collar. Little did they know, Duke's remarkable skill would soon be put to an unforgettable test as they embarked on a seemingly simple day of golfing. Who would have predicted the unexpected twists and turns that awaited them, with each swing on the greens. For now, the morning was still tranquil, the neighborhood was quiet and the lakes at the golf course was calm. However, the daybreak now carried whispers of three friends ready for a day of tee time tales, and fairway adventures had begun.

The First Swing

*D*uane and Bill were the first to step onto the course, ready to take on a deceptively simple challenge: strike the ball with a club and sink it into the hole in as few strokes as possible. What seems straightforward is, in reality, a game fraught with complexities and countless, often hidden, obstacles. The journey begins at the teeing area, commonly known as the "tee box," where the rules are clear and precise. Players must place their ball within this designated space, marked by color-coded tee markers. These markers indicate different starting points, often based on a golfer's age, gender, or skill level. Experienced golfers typically choose markers farther back, while newer players begin closer to the hole. Once a player selects a specific tee color, they are required to stick with that choice throughout the course.

"Where we tee'ing off at today man," Duane asked.

"Make it easy on yourself cuz."

Duke nudged Duane and emitted a low growl.

"OK Duke. It's early, boy. What's going on?" Duane asked, leaning in close. His curiosity piqued after noticing a small portion of Duke's fur standing high. "Hmmm," Duane said. The wrinkles on Duke's forehead raised high as his ears flicked. He stood at attention facing the fairway as if he smelled something peculiar. Duane looked, but saw nothing, and disregarded Duke's warning as a distraction. The two men began stretching their legs and arms, before Bill 'tee'd' up his ball by placing it on a peg called a tee. Tees may be made of wood, plastic or even rubber. Some tees are shaped like a martini glass, and others may have a flat or even spiked head. Either way, the tee helps lift the ball off the ground to ensure the golf ball is placed at the golfer's desired height.

Although Bill couldn't understand Duke's way of communicating with Duane, Bill smiled and admired their interaction. Duane continued stretching and exchanging eye contact with Duke, and Bill went on to select a driver from his golf bag. A driver is a club that allows golfers to typically hit farther. There are endless choices available. Golfers usually strike the ball with whatever club they believe will get the job done.

"OK cousin Bill, show us the way." Duane said before implementing the 'etiquette of silence before a golfer takes a shot' rule.

"It sucks for you to have to follow this," Bill replied with a devious smirk, then took a couple robot like practice swings meanwhile analyzing the course ahead of him.

Duane held back his wicked reply adhering to golf etiquette. Duke stood wide legged, and tail curled. He knew the first soaring ball would trigger birds to scatter. This would be the most dangerous time for Duane because scattering birds could leave fallen feathers. Because some bird wings carry small mites in their feathers, fallen feathers could be dangerous for Duane. Duke was professionally trained as a service dog to sense triggers that could provoke Duane's allergic reaction which would require immediate medical treatment. Duke stayed ready, medical bag around his neck, anticipating any possible reaction from Duane indicating he had come into contact with a particular mite.

Bill unleashed a powerful swing toward the first hole, yards down the fairway. The three stood frozen, their eyes tracking the ball as it rocketed through the air, cracking open the silence of daybreak. But then, as if consumed by an unseen force, a rolling sea fog seemed to rise from nowhere, cloaking the ball and dragging it off course. It landed short of the greens, skidding out of bounds with an ominous splatter. The misstep was a warning: Bill's out-of-bounds shot could severely hinder his chances of staying on par, depending on the rules that applied.

Duane once again held back his sarcasm. He knew golf, after all, is a humbling sport—and today seemed eager to prove it. Behind them, the horizon glowed brightly, but a stubborn morning haze clung to the course, swirling like a vengeful ghost. The men stood motionless, mannequins against the eerie backdrop, absorbing the foreboding beauty of the scene. Bunkers lay scattered across the manicured landscape like hidden traps, while small lakes glinted in the distance. Between the undulating terrain—those subtle rises and dips that could cruelly redirect even the most calculated shots—and the haunting silence, the course was a masterpiece of nature's serenity and man's challenge.

Duane and Bill took a breath, their eyes stretching across the slopes and irregularities that gave the course its captivating allure. Dew shimmered on the fairways, glistening like spectral tears, while long shadows from the morning sun painted the terrain in stark contrasts. The calm of the scene was deceptive, for the beauty before them masked a formidable test of skill and nerve.

When it was Duane's turn to tee off, he approached the course with calculated care. He scanned the fairway, noting the subtle gradients and the lingering mist that added an otherworldly layer to the morning. Standing at the tee box, he felt the cool breeze rolling in from the west. At his side, Duke, his loyal guardian and companion, stood alert, his sharp eyes sweeping the landscape for any signs of danger.

"What do you think, boy?" Duane asked, glancing down at Duke. The dog's ears flicked as his gaze remained fixed on the distant horizon, his tail giving a cautious wag. Duane listened for the wind, gauging it at 15–20 miles per hour, and mentally adjusted his strategy to avoid the same fate as Bill. Kneeling briefly, he studied the green, analyzing its contours and deciphering the terrain's secrets. Duke watched closely, his tail wagging in quiet encouragement as Duane prepared to take his shot.

The challenge lay ahead, veiled in mystery and anticipation, as the course dared its players to rise to the occasion.

"The green slopes slightly downhill towards the west," Bill advised Duane. "Go steady. You may want to aim slightly to the right to avoid my mistake.

Duane nodded, "thanks" and took a long pause. "Well, here goes nothing," Duane said with Duke's tail-wagging, focused on his master's swing. Duane took a steady but swift strike of the ball using his favorite club which is the driver. He slowly followed through his swing afterwards posing in slow-motion. Duke turned to Duane with tongue out and a smiling satisfied expression.

"Nice shot, Duane. Looks like *we're* off to a good start, Bill said with his own sarcastic envy."

Duane grinned, patting Duke's head affectionately. "Couldn't have done it without ma road dog."

"Man, you're killing me. You'd think you're actually having a real conversation wit cho dog," Bill said. "But, let's see how much *your buddy* can help yo ass in the next round."

Now that Duane and Bill tee'd off, they boarded the golf cart to take their second shot. Duke trotted slightly in front of the cart again. As a service dog, Duke's job was to chase away any birds, ducks or other fowl that may be ahead of Duane. Ever-so-often Duke would chase away a raccoon. However, raccoons are night animals and rarely seen in the daytime. Once the golf cart stopped, Duke sniffed around the area to make sure no feathers had fallen where Duane was about to enter.

"Wait a minute... Where's my golf ball?" Bill exclaimed, looking around in confusion.

"Well, it definitely went out of bounds" Duane said. "That's where your ball usually lands."

"Very funny Duane, but last I remember you're the one that can't hit a ball on the green. Just help me look for it."

Duane smirked because hitting a ball out of bounds could cause Bill to lose a stroke, depending on the ball's location and the applicable rule. Although Bill could still have a chance for a *birdie*, if he lost a stroke, staying on par would be a bigger challenge.

In golf, each hole has a specific number of strokes (attempts to get the ball in the hole). That predetermined number of strokes is called a "par." If a person "stays on par," it means they finished that hole in the allotted number of strokes. For example, if a hole is a par 3, and the golfer was able to get the ball into the cup or "hole" in 3 strokes, the golfer shot *par* for that hole. If the golfer completes the hole in one stroke less than the par, that's called a "birdie." If the golfer completes it in one additional stroke for that hole, that is called a bogey and two additional strokes above par is a double bogey.

But before the two could exchange more friendly insults, Duane noticed Duke's posture in a defensive stance. His ears pricked up, and he let out a low deep growl, his attention fixed on something in the distance.

"What is it, Duke?" Duane asked, leaning forward to see what had caught Duke's attention. Suddenly, Duke bolted forward, his instincts kicking in as he raced towards a familiar sight—the mischievous raccoon known to cause trouble in the early morning hours on the course and the critter had Bill's ball.

Raccoons enjoy small eggs and have a tendency to steal the eggs out of bird nests. The paws of raccoons are similarly shaped to human hands. Raccoons even have handprints, and great grip and tactile abilities. Although raccoons are nocturnal animals who are rarely seen in the daytime, it's not always bad or unhealthy to see one in the early morning hours. Sometimes raccoons hunt for food to feed their young at dawn or dusk and sometimes they just actually want a break from the young ones.

As Duke sprang after the raccoon, the chase took on a life of its own. The raccoon darted away with Bill's ball. It went towards the tall trees and thick bushes. Duke was hot on its tail. Duane and Bill followed suit, their laughter mingling with the sounds of their footsteps pounding against the earth.

"Get 'em, Duke!" Duane called out; his voice filled with excitement. Bill grinned, his eyes sparkling with amusement. "Yo boy Duke is no joke," he remarked, enjoying the spectacle before them.

The trio raced across the fairway, their pursuit resembling a scene straight out of a comedy movie. Bill chasing his ball and Duane chasing Duke. They were like kids on a playground, running aimlessly and out of control, determined to keep up with the two four legged animals. The raccoon darted through the underbrush, its masked face and ringed tail, bore a striking resemblance to a bandit on the run. The raccoon scurried desperately to outmaneuver Duke's relentless pursuit. The cunning bandit navigated through the terrain with ease. Its quick reflexes and nimble footwork stayed one step ahead of its pursuers.

After a thrilling chase that seemed to stretch on forever, Duke managed to corner the raccoon near a brick wall. Finally, the sneaky bandit dropped the golf ball and clawed the brick wall like a like a trampolinist leaping through the air. Duke signaled his victory with triumphant bark then grabbed the ball and ran towards the men.

Breathless and exhilarated, Duane and Bill caught up to Duke,

"Well done, Duke!" Duane exclaimed, ruffling Duke's fur affectionately.

Bill clapped Duane on the back, with a wide grin and look of pride on his face.

"That was quite the adventure, wasn't it?"

Duane nodded, still catching his breath. "Absolutely."

"Let's get back and finish this hole before we wake up the entire neighborhood."

The men used their phone to search for the applicable out-of-bound rule online and placed Bill's ball accordingly then continued own with their game.

Summer Swing

With Duke leading the way, the trio made their way back to the green, ready to resume their game with renewed energy and a newfound sense of camaraderie. The men lined up their shots reliving their wild tee off moment that turned into an unexpected wild chase and childlike play. But the day was just getting started.

While the men pondered over how to save par, which club to select, how the terrain varied and whether or not they could "birdie." Duke was attentive to Duane and the environment. He watched Duane's every move.

By the time the gray sky overcast had burned off the two men were teeing off for 4th hole. They were quite far from the club house in either direction, still no other golfers were visible on the course. Although having an empty and wide-open course ahead of them by the 4th hole seemed somewhat peculiar, they were thrilled not to have other golfers behind them rushing their next shot. Especially since they had lost time during the racoon chase and navigating around numerous trap holes of sand on the course, referred to as bunkers. Although bunkers add to the landscape of the golf course, those trap holes can also be "bittersweet". A 'sweet and sour' sauce because at times the shape of the sand trap can sometimes help the golfer direct a shot, thus 'sweet.' But 'bitter' if and or when a ball lands in the *sand trap* i.e., bunker, a golfer may spend extra swings to land the ball back on the greens if not in the hole.

While Bill and Duane were debating about how to take their second shot to avoid their ball landing in a bunker or the lake, Duke had a different focus. He was occupied by the number of wading birds he noticed in the lake, albeit hundreds of yards in the distance. Seeing white birds seemingly standing on top of the water was a different contrast and quite interesting. Duke stood stiff postured, leaning forward, with his ears pinched back. His tail was raised and curled.

Duane did not hear Duke's slow *umph* of noise morph into a low, deep growl, nor did either man see Duke showing his teeth seconds later. Just before his growl, an audible soft breeze hit Duke's nose from a different direction, distracting him from the locked in focus he had on the lake. What Duke could smell was the familiar scent of his owner, though danger was afoot. Just as Duke turned away from the lake, Duane took a shot that skirted along a rim before landing into a nearby bunker. Bill and Duane were frozen but gasped in unison before speaking.

"Great shot buddy," Bill finally said teasing Duane. "There goes *your* birdie."

"Shit," Duane said and slowly turned towards the cart leaving Bill's sinister chuckle behind. As trained and commanded, Duke trotted ahead of the golf cart before herding back towards the rear. He was trained to run away any stray birds that could possibly drop feathers in Duane's path, and trot around the vehicle as if it were cattle. Bill had already taken his shot, though it landed in the fringes. Duane's ball was on the side of the bunker.

When they reached the greens on the 4th hole, Bill was up next to take a shot. Although Duane looked on with respect, he was distracted by thoughts of figuring out how he could manage to get his ball out of the bunker. Duke redirected his focus towards the lake. By now, Duke had a closer view of the lake and the peculiar structure floating. His hair raised on his back—a heighten sign of arousal and aggression.

Bill celebrated his successful shot, his exuberant shout filled the mid-morning air with delight. Duane, impressed by Bill's skill, walked over to him, and offered a pat on the back in good sportsmanship as Bill reached into the hole to retrieve his ball. Despite Bill's recent triumph, Duane couldn't help but feel genuinely happy for his friend, especially since Bill was a few shots behind him.

Meanwhile, Duke, sensing the jovial atmosphere, became distracted away from his gripping gaze on the floating object in the lake. He turned and joined the celebration, setting aside his momentary aggression towards the lake. As the men engaged in playful banter about who would emerge victorious by the end of the game, Bill took the liberty to motion to Duke for a paw handshake.

"Give me 5, Duke. You've got to admit boy, that was a beautiful shot," Bill exclaimed, extending his palm towards Duke. Duke, socially trained, obliged and offered his paw to Bill in return. Bill proceeded to rub Duke's back in appreciation, before reaching to rub Duke's neck under the collar. Duane watched the encounter. His smile faltered as he noticed the emergency bag around Duke's neck was missing. Duane became immediately concerned.

Before he could mention the missing bag, however, Duke surprised him by taking a quick whiff of Duane's crotch. Duane knew not to overreact. Duke often sniffed Duane to test his chemistry for subtle reactions that may be underway. Surprisingly to Bill, Duke stood on both hindlegs and placed one of his front paws on Duane's forehead to touch the perspiration that Duane was emitting.

"What the hell's he doing man?" Bill asked, bewildered by Duke's behavior.

Duke tilted his head, his dark eyes conveying a sense of understanding. With a few quick sniffs, Duke detected a change in Duane's chemistry, his keen senses picking up on subtle shifts in hormones and pheromones.

"Yeah man, you know dogs have an incredible sense of smell," Duane explained, noticing Bill's confusion. "Duke's trained to detect changes in my blood chemistry through my skin. Dogs can sense stress or excitement, just from sniffing skin or breath. I like to think of it as his *superpower*. But you ain't no superhero, so you wouldn't understand."

"Man, shut the fuck up," Bill said with a deep giggle. Nevertheless, Bill still marveled at Duke's remarkable canine abilities. Despite the initial confusion, Duane couldn't help but feel grateful for Duke's keen olfactory senses and instincts, which had once again proven invaluable in detecting the subtlest of changes in their surroundings.

"I'm actually trippin cause I don't see my fuckin medical bag. Look, it's missing! I didn't notice it had fallen off! Did you?"

"You think it could have come off when we were chasing that crazy ass raccoon?" Bill asked.

"Probably so." Duane replied. "Hey Duke, where's Rover? Where's Rover, boy?"

"Um, what the hell is Rover?" Bill queried.

"Remember that red bag around Duke's neck? That's what we call it—the emergency bag with my medicine in it. I use it for allergic reactions. It has my pills and injectables in there."

"Oh yeah, that's right, man. I forgot about that. You haven't had one of those reactions in a minute though, right?" As the two men debated over Bill's recollection of the medical bag, oblivious to their surroundings, a short-legged creature emerged from the lake camouflaged by the dry brush. Only the large white wadding bird perched on the reptile's body was visible.

Wading birds are a type of bird that typically have long legs and long necks, allowing them to wade through shallow water in search of food, such as fish, insects, and crustaceans. Southern California has a variety of wading birds living in wetlands. Some are becoming endangered due to climate change.

One interesting behavior that wading birds exhibit is perching on top of alligator bodies. This behavior may seem unusual at first, but it serves a purpose for both the birds and the alligators. For the birds, perching on top of alligators provides them with a safe and elevated vantage point from which they can survey their surroundings for potential prey. By being higher up, they can spot fish and other small animals more easily, increasing their chances of catching a meal.

For the alligators, having wading birds perched on top of their bodies can provide them with some relief from parasites, such as ticks and leeches, that may be present in the water. The movement of the birds on alligators' backs can help dislodge parasites, providing the alligators with a form of natural pest control.

Overall, the relationship between wading birds and alligators is an example of mutualism, where both species benefit from their interactions with each other. The birds get a safe vantage point, while the alligators get potential relief from parasites and some pest control assistance.

Duke remained ever vigilant, and quick to react. He spotted both creatures through the brush. He could see the alligator's rugged bumpy exterior, covered with scales, mud, and vegetation. As it moved, the skin shimmered in the rising sunlight. Several white feathers stuck onto the alligator's skin. With a ferocious growl and his hair bristling, Duke hurled himself towards the lake, his powerful muscles propelling him forward with determination. But before he could reach the water's edge, Duane's commanding voice rang out.

"Duke, come back!" Duane called, his tone firm but filled with concern.

Reluctantly, Duke obeyed his master's command, his momentum immediately halted as he turned on his heels and trotted back to Duane's side. Neither Duane nor Bill noticed the alligator. Though Duke's instincts had driven him towards the danger, his loyalty to Duane was unwavering, and he returned without hesitation at his master's call.

"It's ok, boy. That bird is too far to endanger me. I'm good." Duane yelled in an assuring tone while Duke ran towards him in return. "Good boy, Duke, good boy." Neither could predict the strange events that loomed.

The Shank

D uane, trusting his dog's obedience training headed towards the bunker to continue his drive towards the 4th hole. His small two shot lead was now in danger since his ball had landed into the sand. Duane figured it would take a couple shots to make par on the hole.

The bunker on the 4th hole had a high slope on the side facing the men giving it a deeper appearance. Duane seemed to suddenly disappear. While Duke ran in Duane's direction, towards the bunker's slope. Bill caught a glimpse of the alligator still crowned by the wadding bird. He couldn't believe his eyes.

Bill's legs trembled in fear. Suddenly, the mysterious alligator, lumbered onto the land with menacing speed, it felt like a scene straight out of an action-packed thriller. The gator was rapidly making its way towards the men's golf cart.

Bill, though not the bravest soul, was very smart and quick at math and statistics. He possessed a sharp mind honed by years of crunching numbers and analyzing stats. Bill believed his chances of making it to the golf cart safely were better than what would happen staying on the green turf. In this moment of peril, Bill's heart raced like an out-of-control skier as adrenaline surged through his veins in a "fight to flight" reaction.

Beads of sweat formed on his forehead, trickling down his face. Each drop seemed to carry with it a mixture of excitement, fear, and suspense.

The fight-or-flight response is a natural physiological reaction that occurs in response to perceived threat or danger. When faced with a stressful or threatening situation, the body releases hormones such as adrenaline and cortisol, which prepare it to either confront the threat (fight) or flee from it (flight).

Duke, ever the loyal companion, felt the weight of the moment pressing upon him as the alligator surged menacingly towards Bill and the bunker where Duane had vanished. Panic threatened to overwhelm him as he grappled with the decision: fight the reptile surging or search desperately for his missing owner?

Canines, like Duke, possess remarkable cognitive abilities, capable of rational thought and problem-solving. Bred by a "Silver Medal Rottweiler Breeder" and trained by the best in Southern California, Duke had been prepared for many challenges, but facing down an alligator was uncharted territory. Despite his training, the urgency of the situation left him little time to plan.

With Bill slowly inching closer towards the safety of the golf cart, Duke's instincts were to defend his owner, not Bill. Yet, the scent of Duane's danger hung heavy in the air, a reminder of the urgent need for medical intervention. Duke's keen senses detected the telltale signs of Duane in the midst of an allergic reaction. Duke knew time was of the essence.

Duke stuttered stepped while thinking about the missing medical bag from his neck. His training taught him the need to have it at this time for his master. Duke's heart pounded. Bill looking on could see that each passing second was like an eternity as Duke struggled with the impossible choice: risk his own safety to confront the alligator or race to Duane's side without the lifesaving bag he needed. Duke's unwavering loyalty to his owner Duane propelled him forward, determined to do whatever it took to ensure Duane's safety and survival.

Meanwhile Bill began looking on from the golf cart in sheer terror. He was frozen though hands trembling to turn the key as he frantically attempted to start the golf cart. However, the key just wouldn't turn and the alligator was looming dangerously closer and closer. Finally, Bill managed to turn the key, but the golf cart's engine sputtered and coughed and simply wouldn't start. Bill realized he was trapped; helplessness and panic gripped his heart. Time seemed to slow to a crawl as Bill's mind raced, desperately searching for a way out of this nightmare. He felt trapped like he was suffocating but knew he had to come up with a plan to save his friends.

"Duane must have had a reaction," Bill thought to himself. Bill reflected on their early morning venture into the brush. But with each passing moment, the alligator's presence grew nearer. Even the sound of the gator's footsteps drew nearer.

"Rover Duke. Rover! Get Rover," Bill shouted. He wanted to redirect Duke's focus on finding the medical bag. If Bill could stave off the gator long enough for Duke to find the medical bag Duane would have a chance to survive Bill thought.

Duke barked at Bill as the engine finally turned over in the vehicle's engine. Seeing Bill drive the golf cart towards the gator was reassuring, but Duke's anger and instinct lured him towards the alligator to fight. Duke was snarling and foaming with aggression as his strong muscular shoulders propelled his legs to confront the open-mouthed beast.

Bill did not want to bear witness to a dog and alligator brawl. Bill knew he could not stomach the carnage he began to envision. The aftermath would be unspeakable.

"No!" Bill shouted with every ounce of breath remaining. "Duke, NO. Rover, Duke Rover."

Alligator Aftermath

"*9*11, what's your emergency?" The receiver on the other end answered routinely.

The call sputtered. Every other syllable was static or not transmitted.

"You're calling an emergency line. If this is not an emergency, please hang up." The dispatch operator said kindly.

"Can you hear me? Can you hear me now?" Bill asked frantically. "This is an emergency. I'm at…"

"I can hear you now, sir. Tell me your name and where you're located in case we disconnected."

"I'm at Willow Springs golf course! There's an alligator loose on the grounds and I have a…"

"There's what? Did you say alligator sir?"

At the same time that Bill was speaking with the emergency operator, JJ in the club house noticed a banner at the bottom of the TV screen. "BREAKING NEWS" interrupted the TV program that had been on. JJ had placed the TV on mute because he needed to call several golfers to reschedule their tee time. It was rather odd; the whole morning golfers had cancelled. He had seen enough of the same recycled news and was tired of watching the same report about the crowds of people waiting in front of the park's lake for a glimpse of the alligator on TV, so he put the volume on mute. However, now a new news report of warnings was in progress. The journalist was giving a report about Reggie Jr. but this time the report appeared urgent and concerning.

"Again, everyone in the Irvine vicinity is being asked to avoid going outside alone. We have reason to believe a slew of exotic animals have been illegally released into the neighborhood," Mayor Green reported. "There's no need for panic, the animal search and rescue division have everything under control. But out of an abundance of caution, we're placing the city on lockdown. Everyone is asked to shelter in place and report anything unusual to the number we're providing."

"Oh, that's why everyone cancelled this morning", JJ thought out loud. "This world is getting crazier every day." Just then a fire truck and paramedics pulled up in the parking lot. While JJ was running outside to greet them, he remembered Bill and Duane were on currently on the course.

In the same moment, down on the 4th hole Duke was emerging out of the lake gripping the red Rover medical bag. Wet and determined, Duke charged towards the bunker where Duane was last seen. In an instant, Duke had spotted the Rover bag floating in the water and immediately ran into the lake to retrieve it. Although the alligator had suddenly retreated, Bill, still in the golf cart on the phone with the dispatch operator was nervously explaining the current situation. Bill believed either his desperate yelling, Duke's growling, or the golf cart's engine somehow scared the gator, given all the loud noises. Not to mention all the metal clubs Bill sent hurling at the reptile.

"Good boy, Duke, good boy. Go boy, go!" Bill shouted with relief when he saw Duke heading out of the lake.

Grass, mud and water flew around Duke's path as he surged towards the bunker. Each powerful stride flexed his 125 lb. muscular build that propelled him up and over the slope to where Duane was. Sand flew as he surged over the top into the sand hole. Once over the hill, Duke found Duane lying in the sand wet with sweat on his face. He was awake, lying on his side holding his ankle and shaking from pain and red with hives on his face due to having a reaction.

Duane stared at Duke several seconds as if in a daze before responding "Oh, thank God. Thank God. Good boy! Good boy." Duke dropped and nudged the Rover bag to Duane. Duke used his nose and nudged the bag closer to Duane in encouragement for him to grab it and open. Duane looked at the bag and slowly opened it.

Duke barked aggressively in encouragement. Duane was not able to raise his voice any higher through the deep rapid breaths and pain in his ankle. Duke barked continuously as if letting Duane know danger was afoot on the other side of the bunker's crest.

Understanding Duke's communication, Duane finally opened the Rover bag with Duke barking and onlooking. Duane opened the medicine package finding the EpiPen wrapped in a sealed box. He proceeded to open it and self-administer the injection of epinephrine using the pen like ampule.

The allergic reversal took effect in a matter of seconds. Duke stood loyally over his master, wagging his tail in approval. But the rescue was not done until Duane was safely out of the bunker. Duke planted his paws firmly in the sand. With a determined grunt, he lowered his head and locked his jaws onto the fabric of Duane's clothing. Duke's muscles strained as he began to pull his master with all his might.

Bill was standing on the other side waving for an ambulance driving swiftly across the greens without sirens or lights. Once he was assured the paramedics saw him, he ran into the bunker by his friend's side.

"Don't move Duane. Just stay still, bro. Paramedics are here," Bill said speaking, still nervously, through sighs of relief.

"What the fuck? Man, I must'a passed out," Duane moaned, then tried to move. "Shit, I think I fucked up my ankle, too. Damn!"

"Just chill, man. I got you. Don't even try to talk. The paramedics are here." Bill spoke softly fighting back tears with words of comfort to his friend.

Several men and a woman climbed out of the fire truck without haste. One of the paramedics, who appeared to be the most senior, approached the two men first.

"We'll take it from here." The chief paramedic spoke to the men with compassion, professionalism and authority then directed the team to proceed assisting Duane. Duke ran down to grab the Rover bag that had rolled down the bunker's hill and handed it to the only female paramedics on the team.

"Smart dog, there," she said dressed in a dark blue suit, white shirt, and fully equipped with a utility belt that seem to weigh more than she. Her long blond hair was neatly pulled back in a ponytail with a few dainty curls bouncing as she moved. A much younger-appearing paramedic, dressed in similar cargo pants and white shirt, with an identification badge labeled 'student,' stood attentively close by, following directives.

Bill grabbed his chest, still recovering from the drama and gave Duke his props.

"He's actually the hero of the day. I'd've drove off in the golf cart and left both of 'em here with that damn gator, if Duke hadn't come outta the lake with ma boy's medical bag." While the team laughed, Duane looked on with seemingly uncharacteristic calmness while the team loaded and strapped him to a stretcher.

Duke stood by dutifully while the team loaded Duane into the ambulance. The chief motioned for the two to ride in a separate truck, and Bill followed suite. But Duke darted away momentarily after he noticed a muddy white feather stuck on the grass, left by the alligator when it had briefly emerged on land. Duke ran towards the feather but the fire chief verbally commanded Duke to return to the truck and Duke was obedient leaving the muddy feather behind.

As the ambulance raced away from the once pristine 4th hole at Willow Springs Golf, the scene that was left behind was a stark contrast to the manicured landscape which the men had tee'd off on earlier that morning. Skid marks marred the once perfectly trimmed fairway. The aftermath of the alligator's presence was evident in the muddy debris scattered haphazardly across the landscape, remnants of its emergence from the lake.

A trail of Duke's paw prints, and mud was imprinted on the greens. Duane and Bill's golf clubs, discarded in defense, lay strewn about like forgotten relics from the Hunger Games. As the ambulance drove towards the club house, tire marks crisscrossed the grass, marking its path. Sand from the nearby bunkers mingled with the mud, and amongst the debris, a plastic wrapping from the EpiPen fluttered in the breeze, a small but poignant reminder of the life-saving measures that had been taken amidst the chaos.

The Emptied Scorecard

*D*uane was discharged from the hospital after an examination and work-up. Doctors ruled out any broken bones due to Duane's fall into the bunker at the time he passed out from the allergic reaction. While in the ER, Duane had to undergo various tests and x-rays because he had momentarily lost consciousness. Doctors needed to make sure Duane didn't suffer a heart attack or stroke. When a person has reduced blood flow, depending on a lot of other factors, vital organs including the brain and heart don't receive vital nutrients and oxygen necessary to work properly. In Duane's case, the temporary loss of blood and oxygen to his brain caused him to have amnesia.

Amnesia is a condition described as a loss of memory. While many times amnesia may be temporary, there are times the loss of memory may last longer than a few seconds, moments, days, weeks or even sometimes months or years. The doctors did not realize Duane had amnesia because he was able to respond appropriately to basic questions. Duane answered correctly when asked his name and birthdate. He also had appropriate interactions with nurses and staff. Duane knew he had been playing golf with Bill who was "waiting outside the emergency room with his dog." There were no visible injuries to Duane's head, aside from sand in his hair. He denied having any further leg pain, and the x-rays failed to show any broken bones.

The ER staff was either more consumed with Duane's extraordinary "tee-time tale and alligator encounter" or his social media stardom, than questioning anything else to access his mental acuity. Once one of the nurses recognized Duane as Mr. Goodbar, it was a wrap. A crowd of staff members lingered around to catch a glimpse or an ear full. Several nurses and staff gathered in a hushed circle, exchanging excited whispers about their experiences at one show or another where they had seen Mr. Goodbar in action. With flushed faces, they eagerly shared how they had cheered him on, some even lucky enough to get called on stage for an unscripted intimate interaction. Their envy was palpable. None of them were shy about confessing the generous tips they had showered on Mr. Goodbar, a token of appreciation for the raw sensuality he brought to life under the stage lights.

Eyes wide with disbelief, lip-biting, jaws dropping in stunned excitement, gasps and covered mouths punctuated the air as the women eagerly recounted their memories. Their faces mirrored the sheer thrill they felt, the electric atmosphere of that untamed night still crackling in their stories. Each detail sparked a fresh wave of excitement, sending shivers through the group as they relived the moments that left them breathless and aching for more—a contagion that spread from one woman to the next, leaving them all momentarily lost in the heat of the moment—forgetting they were at work in an emergency room.

The doctor treating Duane stumbled upon the gossip session and could hardly believe his ears. He was stunned to witness such accomplished and professional women indulging in these playful stories with such enthusiasm. Though part of him was intrigued and his ears burned with curiosity, he knew he couldn't condone the scene. Trying to maintain decorum, he cleared his throat, breaking up the huddle by directing one of the nurses to call Duane's wife, Genie.

The physician, eager to regain control and shift focus back to treating the sick and injured, wasted no time. After a brief conversation with Genie, he discharged Duane home with a clean bill of health. The instructions were straightforward: "You are discharged home. Follow-up with your primary care doctor and allergist." Duane was released home with basic post-visit precautions and a refill order for his EpiPen. The official diagnosis read "resolved allergic reaction" and "mild ankle sprain," the latter treated with a simple stretch bandage, to be used only if swelling occurred.

"Bro, we're so lucky that damn gator didn't try to attack and bite us. I was afraid Duke would get into a fight with that fool and get seriously injured."

"I'm glad I didn't see what was happening to you two on the other side of the bunker. That sound like some crazy shit to me. Gotta admit I'm lucky ma boy Duke is so smart and loyal, though." Duane admitted.

"And we lucky alligators are naturally afraid of humans and anything larger, because we could've been reptile dinner tonight. That's what made me start throwing the golf clubs at 'em. You should've seen how that son-of-a-bitch just turned and slithered his ass back into the water."

"That's too funny."

Bill looked curiously at Duane as he pulled up to Duane's house. Bill noticed Duane didn't have any look of recognition as they approached his block, let alone in front of his home. Bill scratched his head and looked at Duane curiously.

"Bro, you gettin' out the car or what?"

"Oh yeah, get out here?"

"Nah man, you ain't gotta get out here. But I'm going home," Bill said sarcastically. "Now get yo black ass outta the car. You need me to pull up in the driveway or somethin'. You aight?"

"Yeah, no. Nah man, I'm good. C'mon Duke. He puttin' us out."

Duane's vague responses were a little different from his usual animated personality which Bill knew over the years. But Bill attributed Duane's behavior to the traumatic ordeal they had just experienced. Bill noticed Duane fumbled for his keys as he started getting out of the car.

"You sure you gone be good alone bro? What time does Genie get home?"

"Oh," 'Genie?' he thought, scratching his head in a moment of forgetfulness, "I'll be aight. I just realized I don't have my keys to the house." Duane didn't want Bill to know he wondered who Genie was and pivoted to searching for his keys.

"Aw man, they must've fell out in the bunker when you passed out. I'll call Willow Springs and have JJ check to see if someone found them and turned them in. Both of us left our golf clubs behind anyways. I'll call and have 'em delivered."

Duane fumbled more as Bill sat with the car running anxiously.

"Good thing you got that app to open your garage door, right!"

"Oh!" Duane paused, then connected with the word app. "Yeah, right." He looked at his phone and swiped a couple of times before finding the garage door app. His phone didn't require a code.

Instinctively, Duane simply tapped the "open door" link on the phone's app and the garage door immediately opened.

Duke jumped out of the back seat and ran to the tree trunk in sight to relieve himself while Duane slowly walked into the garage, tapping his phone once again to close the door. Bill stayed in the car a few moments longer, before pulling off. He had Genie's cell number in his phone and called her. Another woman's voice answered.

Bill called the correct number but was told Genie was unable to answer the phone because she was evaluating crime scene evidence inside a "fume hood." He left a message for the lab assistant to inform Genie that Duane and Duke *'were home safe.'*

With a heavy sigh of relief, Bill turned the corner to head home himself. He was eager to put the stressful day behind him to prepare for an early flight to New York the next day. As he drove away, he couldn't shake the feeling that there was more to the day's events than met the eye. A lingering sense of unease flickered like the flame of a candle, casting shadows of forgotten memories that would soon reignite—a tale of romance waiting to be rekindled like the next tee time beckoning beyond the horizon.

Part II

Candlelight Dreams

This letter, a candle, my prayer
May the smoke from the flame write my dream
As the love of my life breathes, it's scent
Enlighten and reveal these lyrics meant

Though one breath may cease this burning flame
My love will flourish still the same
Then the stars will know my one desire
That for me you likewise burn a fire.

*D*uane walked into his home, disoriented. He didn't know which room to go to and had no recollection of the surroundings around him. He'd had an incredibly eventful morning earlier at the golf course, but didn't yet realize he had amnesia. As he walked through the house, the feeling of unfamiliarity loomed over his steps. He wandered through rooms, trying to understand why he was in an unfamiliar place.

Duane resolved to following Duke through the house who led him through a hallway to his floating bed that sat in the corner the main bedroom. A portrait hung at the entrance of the bedroom. Duane stopped to take note of its presence. The portrait was Duane embracing a bride elegantly gracing a shimmering white Cinderella dress. The woman's smile gushed and illuminated her deep caramel-colored muscular shoulders that supported a thin oval face radiating fresh spring-like innocence. Duane stopped cold in his tracks.

"Oh! That's me! Gawd, who is that beautiful woman though. She is damn fine. I can't believe I don't know who she is!" he said aloud in shock and disbelief. The portrait was an obvious wedding picture. He grabbed his head between both palms gazing at the photo as flashes of his wedding day flickered through his mind. But the memories were still hazy as he stood.

After several seconds, Duane walked into the bedroom. A large deep blue velour robe was slung over a white barrel chair. He stood in his tracks scratching his head. He went to one of the dresser drawers to find a drawer of watches.

"Oh, these are nice!" He said out loud. "What the…" and entered slowly, taking note of the toiletries, plush towels and decor. As he slid his fingers across the cool tile, an aroma of wood, the feeling of summer, the sound of hip hop and R&B, and scenes of his college days flooded his mind.

Each moment new memories emerged. First, the heat from the shower triggered the feeling of grass under his feet; he could smell the grass and dirt, followed by flashbacks of him in a football uniform, as a kid running on a football field. He saw Bill running with him. For a moment, the distinct taste of sweet potatoes tickled the tip of his tongue, while recalling his mother and father at the dinner table. Chicken, cornbread, greens. He opened his eyes to adjust the knobs on the shower panel while flashes of bongos played in his ear, concerts and music festivals, in a flash. Now, heat from the shower's steam obscured the blue and green marbleized wall. He stepped inside. The water was blazing. The soap, a wood aroma. A loofa hung on the shower panel unlocked the moment he wanted that girl.

Duane thought about the girl in the portrait and recalled the moment his fellow high school seniors were blowing up social media about the superlative votes for their class; *the best for* that, the *most likely person to* this, the *most likely person to* that. At that time, Duane was the hottest guy on campus. He was voted high school homecoming king. But to his surprise Genie's performance during a dramatic reading had gone viral. At the time, Duane wanted to see Genie perform and stepped into one of the after-school drama sets to see for himself why she had suddenly become so popular. As he walked in, Genie was at the mic delivering an intense monologue. Not a rap, not a song. Just a passionate monologue that everyone was holding up their cellphone recording or streaming live.

Genie didn't have on any makeup. No eyelashes, no extensions or weave. She wore her own natural hair is a stylish messy self-made hairdo. Kinda curly, shoulder length, sorta neat, sorta messy but overall cute. No music, no drums, no beat. Just Genie at the microphone, spitting a rhythm that entranced student onlookers. Duane had walked in just as Genie stepped to the microphone stand. She stood. So sincere, so genuine. Genie sounded as if she spoke in someone else's voice. It didn't sound like Genie at all. Suddenly, Duane's mind was flooded with the memory of Genie's entire monologue from that moment.

"Home Sally already knew his favorite color. She's worked on the design all summer, even practiced the timing of her flicker. Huh, there's no way that "girl next door," was going to rain on ma parade. I'll just show her *my* glory. *My* voice: The song of the ocean, a mysterious call to the curious seaman."

Duane remembered a clause in the monologue. Then he recalled a moment of silence and how phones were raised up in the air recording. Seconds later the speaker went on in a musical lyrical beat. Her tempo totally changed. She just switched it up and went:

"So, I took a walk in the summer night, on the beach. Sorta cleared my mind. I walked on the pier and strolled along the shore. A familiar shadow before me. The night was so beautiful and calm. The moon seemed to light up the ocean floor. I wanted to run to his arms but decided to savor the moment instead. After all these years."

Duane felt a wave of familiarity wash over his body as he remembered the monologue—perhaps it was the mention of the ocean during his shower, or the memory of a summer night. All the words to Genie's monologue came back to him ever so poetically he recalled Genie speaking:

> "I gazed at the stars
> From beneath their light
> And dreamed of the day
> I would capture the Knight.
>
> My waters are deep
> I'm an ocean of love
> Still with my patience,
> Though anxious all above.
>
> The knight is a golden and dark shining armor
> Whose eyes once overlooked the horizon.
> I was not his plane view
> Thirst caused his pursuit.
> But just cause you lead, don't mean he'll drink.

Sea divers search for a treasure
In waters not common to man.
A knight of mystical height shall seek
Though his intent were but to wet his feet
He'll lay eye to eye with a jewel he'll forever keep."

Duane recalled that instead of clapping, the crowd of students snapped their fingers. It was after Genie's dynamic monologue, Duane approached her to ask if she'd be his prom date. But Genie flatly turned him down. He remembered his mother's advice at the time.

"When one girl says 'no' know nine others will 'say yes.' Be respectful son, you don't want anyone disrespecting your sister. Treat others the way you want to be treated."

Although Duane was disappointed and stunned, that day he congratulated Genie on a beautifully performed monologue then left the auditorium to go shoot some hoop.

Now, nearly eight years later, the memory of Genie surged through Duane like a warm, lingering caress, igniting every nerve with a potent, familiar heat Duane only felt when he thought about Genie. Now, in the shower, the girl in the portrait was *his ocean*. He could feel her soft lips, taste her tongue on his, recall the dip in her back, feel the wave of her soft round booty. He saw the little dimples over that cute lil booty. He remembered how lovely her breasts dangled on his chest. Her warm, wet ridges vibrating while inside her. His joy began spilling over and over with the flood of memories of Genie and her passion. As Duane remembered, he didn't want the memory of making love to the woman he embraced in the photo to end. He never wanted it to end. As the water trickled over his body, he remembered Genie's face when he surprised her with a special poem he wrote her and recited on their wedding night:

Against the wall, in the sizzle
Cause the heat started a wave
Over wood pinned on the floor
Without stopping, 'til no more
Then a mirage crept in my sleep
At last, a thirst quencher, oh so sweet!
As I washed my face in your thick, sweet stream
You're my fantasy, and everything I dreamed.

Duane remembered how Genie blushed. But in this moment tears came to his eyes because he unexpectedly remembered his graduation day. The moment both parents hugged and congratulated him. Duane began to feel abrupt pain the back of his head as he suddenly remembered a scene of paramedics and lights flashing. Then flashes of the memory of him waking up in the hospital with tubes in his nose and arm. Another flash of the recollection of his father lifeless in a coffin and his mother's expressionless face immediately forced Duane to his knees on the shower's marble seat. He began to sob. It all came back to him. His life, his love. His pain, his joy, his passion. That moment in the shower, he remembered who he was. Like a door opening to planet earth, he arrived. Duane was back.

He stepped out of the shower, dried off, then wrapped himself in the blue robe and tied a knot. His cell phone rang as if on cue. He answered.

"Duane, are you okay? How do you feel?" Genie, on the other line asked. Her voice was filled with concern.

"Genie?" Duane said with exhaustion, and a tremble in his voice. "I remember… I remember you!"

"Um, you remember? You remember what, babe."

"I remember you!" Genie was silent while Duane fumbled. He didn't want to alarm Genie nor let her know he had forgotten who she was and that he just remembered, moments ago, that he was married to her.

"You remember what, babe?" She repeated. "Duane, can you hear me?"

"Uh, yes, bad connection. What time did you say you're coming home?" Duane said, walking out the bathroom to gaze at their wedding portrait again.

"Well, first, I wanted to check on you. How you feeling? How's your ankle? Are you in any pain?"

"My ankle, oh, yes, it's um, not broken and I'm fine. No need to worry about anything at all. I'm good."

"Are you sure? You're not faking, are you?"

"No baby, I'm good." Genie wasn't exactly convinced.

"What about Duke? You guys eat yet? I might be a little late coming home. Thanks to you and Bill we may have a breakthrough in the case I'm on."

"The case?" Duane was confused. Not only did he not know what kind of case Genie was talking about, it also took a moment for him to remember what her job was.

"Oh! Yes, the case. That case. Ok, baby, um, you just keep working. Me and Duke are fine. I'll, um, fix something for dinner. Should I make enough for you, too?"

"Very funny. You know you always cook for the 3 of us."

"The 3 of us?!" Duane said alarmed, and swiftly walked through the house to see if there was anyone else living there he may not have remembered. '*Oh lord, do we have a kid I forgot about or something?*' he thought looking through the other bedrooms, and taking a long pause. Duke, perched up on a luxury doggie cushion sprang up at attention when Duane entered. "What are you thinking you wanna have tonight?"

"Don't worry about me, I had a late lunch. I don't think we ran out of ground beef for Duke so, you two go ahead and eat without me tonight."

Duane took a sigh of relief, but he was surprised. '*You mean I'm cooking for a dog too?*' He asked himself. Then he looked in the mirror passing one of the smaller bathrooms, '*I must be a great guy, cooking for a goddamn dog.*' "Baby, just focus on work. Me and, um, Duke are just fine," looking over his head at the dog. Duke was walking right by his side. "Yes, I'm...we're both just fine. I think I'll turn in early tonight though. Don't be surprised if I'm sleep when you come home. We had a long day."

"You, in bed early? That's different. But ok, I understand. I know I'd be exhausted, too, if I had to face Bill and an alligator in one day," she said with a soft chuckle.

After hanging up with an '*I love you*' to each other, Duane sat on the couch reflecting on the moments he recalled at the hospital. He was thinking about the nurses, techs and staff, amazed at the thought of an alligator encounter at the golf course when his phone rang. It was Bill. He thought about not answering, but Duke was staring at him with such intensity, he had no choice.

"Hello."

"Hey, man" Bill said with a happy sound in his voice. "You keel over yet," then let out a chuckle. "How you feeling, man? You good?"

"Man, I don't choke at the first sign of danger like you."

"Man, fuck you. I should've let your punk ass rot in the bunker," Bill said affectionately. "I was concerned about you and wanted to make sure you good, though." While Bill went on a rant, the words 'keel over' triggered yet another flashback for Duane.

He remembered how he and a group of guys were locked in a tie during a community basketball game at the gym. He and the guys were at the Santa Monica gym. A place where young men took out their week's aggression on the court and left it all there. It was a simple community gym, that's been open to the public for years. Many locals took advantage of the facility, but it was not uncommon people outside the neighborhood would use it too.

There are a few rules of engagement when it comes to local basketball pick-up games. Most people live by the unwritten rule of an honor system. While most guys were relatively honest about rule violation calls, there was always an occasional nut or two who would manage to mess up the vibe with unnecessary arguing on each call.

That evening, as Duane recalled one of the games, he remembered the time a strange bird had managed to fly into the gym. Most of the guys ignored the bird, but the darn thing couldn't find its way out and stayed inside spooking the guys' shots, so many claimed interferences. The game turned into comedy until the moment Duane began coughing violently and grabbing his throat. No one knew what had happened, except Matt. Duane's face was swollen and riddled with hives; he was wheezing when Matt, his teammate, received Duane's pass. Matt held the ball and stopped the game.

The guys thought it was a joke or another bogus interference call until Duane doubled over.

"Tell the office to call 911," Matt shouted. "Duane, you're having an allergic reaction!"

"Allergies?!" Lorenzo cried foul. "Man, that big fool is allergic to losing. He's faking this shit. Get up man!"

But when Lorenzo looked at Duane's face and saw the swelling, he became fearful. Lorenzo immediately ran to the office with untold urgency. The paramedics were down the street and quickly made their way to the gym just after Duane fell to the ground. Matt immediately jumped into action and started performing chest compressions on Duane. Once the paramedics arrived inside, an oxygen mask was placed, and an injection of adrenalin was administered.

Duane held the phone remembering the entire life-threatening event as Bill was on a two-minute rant about his six-iron that was left behind at Willow Spring golf course.

Everyone had blamed Duane's reaction on excessive dust and dirt particles in the gym. Some joked about 'stank cologne Boo wore' or something Duane had eaten before going to the gym, until it happened again. Six months after Duane and Genie were married, the exact same thing happened again. The men were playing basketball when Duane went up for a shot and was fouled, so the men argued back and forth over the contact. Matt once again noticed Duane's face was red and immediately knew he was having a reaction. This time, Duane had an EpiPen, but the device was on the bleachers in Duane's jacket pocket. By the time the paramedics came everything was under control, thanks to Matt. But as the paramedics were leaving someone noticed a similar white bird as the one 6 months ago.

Extensive testing confirmed Duane's allergies to bird mites. But an outside specialist determined the type of mite had to have come from a very specific and unique breed of bird not typically seen in the area. The specialist didn't think much of it. It was Genie's persistence with requests for genetic testing and an entomologist referral that nailed the diagnosis for Duane. At first Duane was irritated by Genie's constant inquiries and research into the matter. He regretted that day even going to play basketball after practically completely giving up the sport for golf. However, Genie didn't appreciate golf as an exercise, and he had missed seeing the guys he used to play with. Against Duane's better judgment, he saw the specialist Genie recommended.

Bill interrupted Duane's silent recollection, "so they'll probably deliver them to your house tomorrow... You there, can you hear me?"

"Oh, yes, the call was a little choppy," Duane lied. He was deep in thought while Bill was talking. Duane, regretting having to lie to his friend. He took great pride in being honest and just telling the truth.

"I can hear you man. Can you hear me? Bro, you ok?" Duane took a long pause. He really didn't want to put his friend at alarm, especially knowing Bill was leaving town. But at the same time, he didn't want to carry on a charade.

"Yeah man, uh, I feel ok. I just realized I have a little amnesia."

"Yeah, I could tell something wasn't right by the way you were answering and acting when you got out the car earlier. The doctors said some things about today might be a little hazy, but all your tests were normal. I asked them. The ER doctor said you may have a little PTSD too."

Duane smiled. He was relieved he didn't have to lie to his good friend.

"So, I'll just pick up my clubs from you when I get back in town. Just focus on getting better. I know ya gurl Genie's all over it. Ain't nothing getting past her 'bout her baby D dub!"

"Fasho, man. You got that right. I just talked to her before you called. I'm sure she asked the doctors a million questions already."

The two men laughed and hung up the phone. Duane closed his eyes for a moment to relive his recollection of his wife in the shower. He thought about the many poems Genie had read to him the first year they were married.

A shadow was seeping through the shutters and illuminated a reflection on the wall. The reflection caught Duke's attention causing him to stand up and face the light. Duane moved his wrist back and forth for the medical bracelet to catch light. He teased Duke with the metal reflection, but the flickering triggered a new flood of memories for Duane.

Tales From the Tee Box

*D*uane continued having memory flashbacks. One such memory Duane recalled was the day Genie had left John Wayne airport to meet him in Florida. Duane had left California a couple days earlier for a business investment meeting in South Carolina. He and Genie were going to meet up later in the week in Florida. The two planned to meet in Orlando to pick up their new puppy. Coincidentally, Duane's friend Marcus lived in Florida. After Duane finished the meeting in South Carolina he met up with Marcus. The two enjoyed golf and decided to enjoy a day on the greens after Duane's work meeting. He and Marcus had been good friends for many years.

"Man, we gotta do Farmstead. It's a little pricey, but well worth it, bro. And, you'll get to say you tee'd off in South Carolina and putted in North Carolina. That's my favorite part; it's right on the border of both. And Bro, I tell you the course is so immaculate, too. Wide open with treelined fairways *and* a few bunker shots for a lil challenge," Marcus said in between bites of chicken wings and stuffing down salted fries. "I checked *The Golf App* last week. Tomorrow's the best day."

"A lil challenge?"

"Well, at least for you."

"Well not everybody can hit the ball as long as you, in the bunker."

"Have you tried *The Golf App?* That's the real gamechanger," leaning over to show Duane on his phone. "Here, look at this one. You get real time weather updates. Not just the temperature and wind, but how much precipitation, and the atmospheric pressure. In real time too, bro!"

"Man, that only makes a difference when you get it ahead of time. It's not like imma stop before a shot and check the weather."

"I'm tryna figure out how to use the app that's supposed to record your swing and play it back. Supposedly other people on the app can comment on your swing and everything."

"Man, forget that." Duane replied emphatically. "I don't need nobody sitting at a desk having nothing to say about what I'm doin'. They can keep them apps, you gotta get out there and hit the fuckin' ball. That's it. I don't need some app telling me what I already know. You gotta be out there and witness the game yourself. Learn how to check the wind. Learn what it feels like to swing and make adjustments. That's what they did before all this smart phone shit. Just play the damn game. The only app I need is in applying my club to the fucking ball." Duane wasn't one to hold his tongue, especially with his closest friends. The two talked golf and basketball, going back and forth in between cheap shots at one another with neither getting offended.

"All I'm saying is, it's a challenging course. It's pretty cool though. You'll love it."

Duane sat in his kitchen and closed his eyes remembering his visit with Marcus just before going to get his and Genie's pup. He thought about how short he'd been with Genie that day when she was trying to get to the airport. He and Marcus were at Farmstead playing with a 16-year-old golfer who was shooting better than both of them. When Genie called Duane that day, he and Marcus were struggling to advance their ball off the fairway. The course had been aerated the week before and was slower than what the men hoped. And to make matters worse, they were playing in the morning before the Carolina breeze and were battling annoying bugs making Duane nervous about having a potential reaction.

Duane had just finished putting when his phone rang with Genie on the other line.

"Babe, I'm trying to get to the airport and got a traffic ticket! By two officers! Not one, but two!! Their lights nearly blinded me, there was this terrible glare, 'cause the was sun setting and I couldn't hardly see. I was on the freeway and didn't even have a safe spot to pull over, cause the road was winding and..."

"Ok, ok, ok. Enough!" Duane said insensitively. "Damn, take a breath. Did you just pull over to the shoulder?!"

"Yes, but they said I took too long to pull over. By the time I saw somewhere safe to stop there was a second police car behind me. Like I was a slow speed chase criminal or something."

"Look, just get to the airport safe. I can't talk right now." Duane said at the time.

"I'm already at the airport, but after the officers pulled me over traffic was backed up a mile long, and the line going through security had a gazillion people in front of me and..."

"Look, I already said I can't talk. You need to get off the phone and pay attention to when you need to board the damn plane. You're doin' too much right now babe."

"OK, but I'm trying to tell you what happened cause..."

"Enough! I can't do this right now. Get off the phone and get on the plane."

Duane sat in the chair at home and rubbed Duke's forehead thinking back at the conversation. Brushing Genie off in her excitement was bad enough, but he knew how much Genie had worked the day before she was to meet him in Florida. And he knew how much she wanted to get the puppy. Even though she insisted the dog was for him to "protect and serve," he also believed he would have enough time to take medication if he had an allergic reaction. Having a puppy was *just one more added burden.*

Duane put his head in his hands thinking. That day he and Marcus played, Duane had told Marcus that Genie was overly emotional, '*a trainwreck over a damn puppy.*' He had even hung up the phone before she was finished talking. Now he thought his attitude was a bit crude that day and wished he could take it all back.

"I already know how that goes. These women be all over the place with their hormones. And if you think that was a lot, just wait 'til she gets pregnant. That's a whole different level!" Marcus said that day to Duane before a bogy, (losing a point on the par).

"She works too much to get pregnant, man," Duane recalled saying before striking his ball around a water hazard and past a bunker near a dry area of shrubbery and weeds. Marcus gloated.

"But honestly, bro, sometimes you gotta just listen and let the woman rant. All the extras are really their way of saying '*I need some attention.*' I been married five years longer than you two. Take it from me, bro. When a woman is on a rant, just shut up, listen, and agree. You'll be the hero in the end."

Duane recalled how Marcus schooled him that day on the joys of marriage. He remembered how he and Marcus played with Kevin, a 16-year-old, that day. The three got into the golf cart towards the next hole. Kevin was quietly making par on each hole and rode in the golf cart in silence until Duane brought him into the conversation between he and Marcus.

"Hey youngsta, how'd you get your game?"

"Huh?"

"Yo game, Bro. You got good game. What you using?"

"Well," Kevin said from the back seat looking up from his phone. "I kinda use physics to plan out my shot. I noticed both of you could use help with your swing."

"Boy shut the fuck up. Ain't not body ask you what the hell you thought about our swing." Duane said to the youngster in jest.

"You can swing this." Marcus chimed in gesturing vulgarly. Trash talking was a ritual for Duane and his friends, a beloved tradition that turned any gathering into a lively, spirited event. The playful shit talking was often sharp and unfiltered, added a layer of fun and flavor to every game they played—a way to bond through humor and shared bravado.

Kevin took a deep sigh and adjusted his spectacles. He'd heard enough from the two that day to understand the men's sense of humor and simply ignored it and held his ground.

"You need to have a good swing with your *shoulders*." Emphasizing the word 'shoulders.' "You guys aren't using your *shoulders* in your swing. Also, you're not rotating your wrists freely," the young high schooler said.

"We oughta put lil man out the cart," Duane turned smiling at Marcus. Marcus slammed for a second on the break, and both men laughed.

"I sure ain't expect the disrespect to come out of 'em like that," Marcus, said driving the four-seat cart slowly forward. He looked over his shoulder with a wide grin at Kevin to make sure he was ok. "You gone have to put yo money up, runnin' yo mouth like that."

"Or shut the fuck up." Both men said simultaneously with a fist bump.

"I know you don't wanna lose yo lunch money out here." The two men laughed. Kevin rolled his eyes. And the three climbed out the golf cart.

Kevin took his shot first. "You have to maintain the shaft like this," he said while positioning his body and holding his putter. He took a couple demonstration swings while daring either of the men to breach golf etiquette by speaking during his shot. "See, look. You have to wait for the right moment to release your wrist so it rotates freely." He took a good sturdy putt sending his ball eight feet where it stopped just short of the cup. The two men looked at each other with disgust and jealously towards the youngster as he took the liberty to place the ball in the hole for a birdie.

"You got that, Duane? You're a south paw, so you gotta reverse it."

"Man, Imma reverse this iron on your head." Duane replied.

"How 'bout you two just get a pressure mat and practice more on your swings."

"Shut the fuck up, both men sung their expletive in perfect harmony. "You don't know shit."

Kevin took a long sigh and burst into laughter before responding sarcastically.

"A pressure mat could be good for y'all. It uses technology to help you adjust how you move and what your patters are. It measures how you transfer your weight and how much pressure you put on the ground, then it analyzes all the data and gives you input on how you can adjust your movements to improve your swing."

Marcus sang Kevin's last statement with playful banter then pretended to be a mean as possible.

"And who the fuck asked you!"

Kevin and Duane burst out into laughter, then Duane took out a pitching wedge to chip on the green. However, he misjudged reading the angle of the green which had undulations causing the ball to roll down and away from the cup onto the 'first cut' and fortunately stop well short of an area with bushes and a bobcat warning sign. First cut is the grass that is slightly higher than the closely trimmed grass along the fairway. Kevin looked away smirking.

Marcus was quiet before taking his putt and did no better. He putt made an "errant shot'—one that significantly misses the golfer's intended target and goes far off course. This is often due to a poor swing or golfer's miscalculation. While Duane remained quiet, Marcus ignored Kevin's smirk but couldn't resist shit talking as Duane approached his ball.

"Man, watch it. Hopefully there ain't no bobcat behind you to take a piece outta you ass. You know we got rattlesnakes here too."

Duane shook his head and spoke loud enough for Marcus and Kevin to hear. "Long as that snake ain't coiled up ready to strike I'm good.' He examined the terrain ahead of him and the hole then took a moment to return the banter. "Our Roadrunners in Cali keep the rattlers in check." He turned and looked over his shoulder as if to search for any signs of a reptile. "When that Roadrunner digs its talons in that mofo, it's a wrap," squatting down to inspect the greens for the surface variance. But Marcus continued his playful bullshit in breach of etiquette.

"Man if I gotta go into the bushes, I'm taking my big iron to whack that mothafucka."

Duane took a well calculated putt that aired a fortune of good luck. His ball rolled around the lip of the cup as Duane leaned hard to the side as if willing his ball a fall-in command. The lean seemed enough for the ball to drop in and Duane to made par to quiet his buddy Marcus and Kevin the wanna-be-prodigy-golfer.

In thinking back on that day, Duane stood in his kitchen reflecting on the talk Marcus had given him several months prior. He looked softly at Duke, rubbing his ears.

"I sure didn't want no puppy. No offense to you boy, but a puppy wasn't what I planned for." Duke rolling over submissively for Duane to rub Duke's belly. "Yeah boy. Good boy. But I guess if it weren't for you, Bill thinks I could have gone into an anaphylactic shock. What'd you think, boy. Is that right? Yeah, good doggie. You went out there to get Rover didn't you boy? Didn't you? Meanwhile that punk ass Bill choked." Duke flopped totally on his back to get the most of his belly rub. "Yeah, that gator would've had some problems if you had to get your jaws on 'em. Ain't that right boy?" Duane rubbed Duke affectionately recalling he and Genie's first year of marriage. He thought about how the two had known each other since high school but ran in different circles.

Duane was popular even while in elementary school. By the time Duane attended high school, he was a popular athlete and well-loved by many students. However, Genie was never impressed with Duane. The two never shared classes together and thus had little contact with one another.

While Genie loved theatre arts, she had her eye on science while in elementary school, and by the time she was in junior high she knew what kind of work she wanted to do. She was a smart, disciplined student with a passion and love for learning. '*My wife is something else,*' Duane thought while reflecting on his '*drama queen wife.*' He thought back to recall another day he stopped by Genie's theatre class to catch another one of her monologues. Since the first time he saw her perform he'd go back to catch another one, every once in a while. He enjoyed listening and seeing her perform. It was after the prom. Duane had taken someone else. The expression "rock yo world" was Genie's theme for her drama class assignment of that week. The assignment for her was to 'spit a beat,' but Genie elected instead of rapping, she'd give a sultry monologue. Everyone loved her monologue once again. Duane believed Genie changed her performance after seeing him walk in the room. She stepped to the microphone and looked straight at Duane and into his eyes, speaking with attitude and purpose.

"Why Would You Want to Rock My World

Why would you want to rock my world
If I'm not the lady you call yo girl.
Why would you want to give me a dream,
When I'm not the woman you call yo queen?

> See, don't even bother to fan *this* flame, encourage my love
> Or even the same,
> As you lay on your side, in the dark of the night,
> and whisper *my love* when she's out of sight

Despite those warm feelings oh, you know wrong from right."
Genie spoke with passion right at Duane. He wondered if all the
students were looking at him as she spoke with her lips nearly kissing
the mic. She took a step closer and continued.

"Still you water my grass and lay under my tree
then soak up the sun and swarm like a bee.
Are you ridding high when you come into town
As if you're the only sharpshooter around?"

'*Shit*,' Duane thought to himself at the time. He reflected about
all the times he stopped by Genie's house and spoke to her father
while he was watering their lawn. Genie was '*killing me softly*,' Duane
thought, like the Roberta Flack song he'd heard his parents play over
and over again, back in the day. Genie went on with her monologue:

"I don't need your music; I don't like your beat
Check yo self fool, I've got a rhythm to keep.
I was born in July, my rainbow is west,
If what you're giving is your true best
Then lace up your shoes, I ain't cast n ma pearls
cause you are not welcome, to walk in my world-
So, …why would *you* want to "rock my world?!"

Genie recited looking right at Duane. She had delivered another
viral performance, and this one seemed to be directed straight at

Duane. In retrospect, Duane wasn't 'mad at her,' after all, it was Genie's commitment and tenacity a couple years ago, that helped doctors narrow down the exact reason for his allergies.

Duane nodded to himself at the memory of his decision to marry Genie. The girl was just as confident as he. Duane went into the kitchen, stood back and paused thinking about the flood of memories coming in.

'This is a beautiful kitchen. Now, when did we move here?' He asked himself while looking at Duke waiting for an answer. Seconds later he recalled when the two did a walk through the day they received the keys after the close of escrow. Duke sat up in a perfect pose looking at Duane while memories played like movie reruns.

"What do you eat boy? Where's your food?"

Duke stood to attention and barked. Duane opened the door to the refrigerator. With the exception of packed and refrigerated dog food, it was nearly bare.

"What the…So you have food here, but I don't?"

Duke barked several times and wagged his tail aggressively. When Duane closed the door, he noticed butter in the front. *Land of Lakes*, and once again a flood of memories took him by surprise, filling in everything he had forgotten about Duke and his food.

A new wave of memories fell upon him. He recalled the day he and Genie were driving in a rental car through Groveland, Florida, after he had left Marcus. The two were going to pick up the puppy Duke. The couple always enjoyed a bit of trivia during their road trips. Duane recalled how Genie enjoyed reading historical bits of information, and the two would alternate asking each other questions while the other would contemplate answers. It was their game of road trivia.

That day in Florida, while the two were trying to guess what type of trees they were passing by, a construction zone slowed them down. Genie read one of the signs and decided to research and look up the purpose of the construction as a trivia question for them.

"Oh, my goodness, Duane. You're right, these are oak trees. But guess what. They're not just any oak trees."

"Um, don't tell me this is where they'd hang a brotha!"

"Ok, see. You need to stop honey."

"Let's be forreal. We in the south! This the *deep* south, babe," looking towards her for a response. "Good thing you not driving."

Genie looked sideways at Duane, pursed her lips and they both chuckled.

"No, but look. We're passing an abandoned cemetery. '*Oak Tree Union Colored Cemetery.*' It's an abandoned African American cemetery. Dating all the way back to the late 1800's. For years, Black folks weren't even allowed in this area!"

"Wow, that's something. We couldn't even be allowed near a cemetery where our own people are buried!"

"But the beauty of it is that the community is coming together to restore it now. There's even a task force! But the files about the people who were buried here was in a box in a barn that got...eaten by rats!"

"Ok babe, please. I don't wanna hear about no damn rats eating up lost files!"

"This is really fascinating," Genie said with an eye for forensics. "I'm surprised I never heard about this site during my fellowship."

"Ok, Genie. Change the subject." Duane said authoritatively. But now, Duane stood staring in the refrigerator months later thinking about the times he spoke to Genie so sternly. '*Afterall*', he now thought. '*Researching details about dead people was part of what she does for a living.*'

Groveland is known for many beautiful lakes and trees. Before 1922 the city was previously known as '*Taylorville,*' after a pair of brothers named Taylor sought to harvest turpentine. Turpentine is an oil used to manufacture soap and some cosmetics. In the olden days some folks used turpentine to relieve pain from blisters, corns, burns and insect bites.

As they drove along, a tapestry of the state's nature unfolded before their eyes and thoughts, as if whispering secrets of a dark past known throughout many areas in the country. The winding road embraced them. It was lined with a myriad of majestic trees whose very presence held stories untold. Genie reflected briefly to share her own family history.

"You know, the summer before my fellowship I researched my own family ancestral history with one of my cousins. We were able to trace my father's side back to our family born enslaved and the first person in our family born free.

"Wow, that's incredible. I really wish I could do mine." Duane spoke with sorry while driving.

The tall proud symphony of trees boasted a vibrant diversity that painted the landscape along the road with a melody of hues. Towering oaks, draped in mossy veils, reached towards the heavens, while magnolias blushed, infusing the air with a delicate fragrance. Genie was tempted to let the window down to wash her hair with blowing wind but resisted to avoid needlessly exposing Duane to potential allergens.

"What is that stuff hanging on the oak trees, Duane?"

"Girl, as smart as you are, don't you know what that is? It's moss. Probably Spanish moss."

"But I'm reading here Spanish moss is actually an herb in the pineapple family! Apparently, the seeds blow on trees, then grows hanging. It's found in a lot in moist climates. Wow. And... of course, birds use it for nests, but look, bats, frogs, spiders and even snakes can be found in it. Ugh, that's a no for me!"

"Definitely swampland."

"Hmmm, look, years ago people use to use it to stuff furniture and mattresses."

"I won't be sleeping in it."

"With your allergies, you probably wouldn't wake up if you did." Genie had a hardy laugh before researching more. "Ah, look, how long do you think oak trees live?"

"Probably at least a hundred years," Duane replied steering around a winding road lined with a myriad of majestic trees.

"Some can live two hundred to five hundred years!"

"Yup, imagine the stories the trees would tell. Hey, you like history and researching. Don't you wanna write a book one day? There's an idea: What stories would southern trees tell?"

"Yeah, that is a good idea honey. Imagine this: if trees had the gift of speech, they'd, recount tales of eras long gone. Tales of generations of humans *and* animals who sought solace beneath their *sturdy* branches!" Genie became animated and theatrical. She held the phone to her lips gesturing as if it were a microphone. "Trees timeworn trunks, etched with the wisdom of ages, and witnesses of human experiences and natural wonders!" She went on and on smiling and admiring her own creativity. Hmmm, how 'bout *tree carvings inscribe ages of human history!*"

"Ok, ok, give you an inch and you take off like a Viola Davis monologue."

"At least I'd receive an academy award for my performance," chuckling. "Where do we get off this road at?"

Duane sat at the kitchen table, staring out the window, watching the final ray of sun dip into dusk. As he reflected on the day's events and the fragments of memory that had returned, he felt a growing discomfort with the person he had been. His impatience and harsh words to friends and his wife, Genie, echoed throughout his mind. He decided not to wait up for Genie. Instead, Duane was determined to be better. He climbed into bed early, hoping that with rest, he could fully reclaim the rest of his memories and reshape his future.

One Day in a Moment

When I miss you one day in a moment
I do more than miss you.
If you ask me, how do I know...

Before I ever, ever even knew your embrace
Recalling your eyes
I wanted to comfort you without haste.

When I miss you, one day in a moment
I feel your hand caressing my shoulder.
It is right there, in that moment,
My desires could simply be no bolder.

That day on our first moment
I took that time to listen to your heart
Inside your warm heart of serenity
I never want to depart.

When I miss you, one day in a moment
I feel your lips passionately kissing mine.
Then, right there, in that moment
I'm craving you, that moment in time

Neatly wrapping my body with yours
Do not ever believe I don't want you inside me.
I only desire for more than an instant, I care!
That when I miss you one day, in moment
I'll awaken, and you'll be right there…

DNA Drive

G enie had been immersed in the investigation throughout the entire day. As a forensic analyst, her job was to review and examine biological evidence collected from crimes. Most of her day was spent comparing DNA from crime scenes and categorizing the evidence according to suspects, witnesses, or persons of interest. Genie evaluated DNA from various sources, including blood, hair, semen, saliva, tissue, fibers, footprints, fingerprints and occasionally urine to extract tissue. Her work days typically consisted of some variation of collecting DNA evidence, appearing in court, and visiting hospitals to interview people involved in various traumas.

She had long since gotten over the Alan fiasco and often didn't even notice him in passing at the courthouse. However, vehicular manslaughter—a homicide (unlawful killing) where someone unintentionally causes a death while driving—occasionally caused their cases to overlap, as Alan's firm often dealt with such incidents.

When Genie wasn't in the field (hospital, court, witness or victim home, or crime scene), she was in a lab. Genie sat in front of a slew of computer monitors. She wore a white disposable jumpsuit, face mask, goggles, gloves, and a disposable hair bonnet. Many of the images Genie needed to look at while working—to compare the

DNA to—would make most people ill or vomit, but Genie enjoyed the depth and challenge of her work.

The lab she worked in contained complicated DNA analyzing machines, designed to evaluate DNA at varying levels. Genie loved working with these machines, despite the on-the-job stress from demanding deadlines. She enjoyed analyzing DNA and had taken many genetics courses during her postgraduate internship, honing her skills and deepening her passion for the meticulous work she performed every day.

Moments after Genie hung up the phone with Duane, she was asked to stay later to go into the field for two interviews. The dispatch team leader informed Genie that she would be part of the crime investigative team to go the home of the child that was *allegedly* bitten by a monkey as reported by the mayor during the press conference earlier that day. Additionally, members of the team were going to a crime scene at Willow Springs Golf Course. The crime scene team is called SOCO, an acronym for "scene of crime officers."

However, after the chief was informed that Genie's husband was coincidental at the *alleged* alligator encounter Willow Springs, he decided to accompany SOCO despite the assignment had been determined earlier. Genie was the only DNA analyst at the division for the moment. Two other DNA analysts were out on leave. The chief wanted to make certain a defense attorney wouldn't argue bias if the case went to trial since she was the only one with DNA analysis credentials. The detectives believed there was a connection between the two *alleged* illegal wild animal incidents.

When a report of a crime hasn't been proven, legal language and journalists reporting apply the term *allege* in front of accusations being investigated pending conviction proved at trial. Detectives had already been investigating reports of strange or possible foreign animals spotted throughout the city. Several neighbors had also reported unfamiliar animal sounds at coming from a particular home. However, without "probably cause" of a crime committed in the home, police were only able to knock on the door to ask questions. Probably cause is a legal standard used by police or law enforcement to justify an arrest, search, or obtain a warrant. It means there is enough evidence or that there is a reasonable belief that a crime has been committed, and the person or place involved is connected to that crime. Since the people at the reported home were not cooperative, police would need to wait until a possible crime were reported and *probable cause* existed. This protection is known as 'the 4th amendment.'

When Genie spoke to a group of kids at a local high school during career day months earlier, she explained several legal concepts to students.

"People have the right to be protected in their home from an unlawful search or seizure by the government, unless the government has legal exceptions to this 4th amendment rule. If there are no exceptions to the rule, then the police search is illegal."

"Can you tell students an example of a police search?"

"Sure. First of all, the 4th amendment doesn't just protect a person from an illegal search in a person's home. People also have the same protection in their car, walking down the street, even things a person may own like even a computer. When the police—or not just the police, say even someone employed by the government—looks into the personal, private things that someone owns, the 4th amendment applies.

"What if it's my locker?" A student asked. Another student giggled.

"This is where there could be exceptions to the 4th amendment. If the locker is at a school or determined to be the ownership of someone else, then it would only apply to the person who has a legal right or ownership. As a student, your locker belongs to the school, if you worked for an employer, for instance, your desk or computer would be the ownership of the person who is the legal owner. Lockers are the property of the school; therefore, schools only need a 'reasonable suspicion' to search the school locker or school's computer."

"Ok students did you hear that. That means you better be careful what you have in your lockers or what you do on the school's computer."

"What about my backpack?" Another student yelled. "Can a teacher search my backpack?"

Genie smiled and said "Assuming *your* backpack, briefcase, computer bag, or cellphone is yours, it's your personal property. The school, teacher or principal had better have a good reason or they could be considered violating your 4th amendment right."

Oh! Students ooed awed, and giggled sparking numerous side conversations and jokes with one another.

"Listen. Listen up everyone. Quiet, quiet. Ok, we'll have to have agent Genie come back to speak to us again. I see she has so many interesting topics to share with us about crime investigation, genetics and law," the teacher said in effort to tamp down student's conversations sprawling between themselves.

Genie was informed SOCO was going to Willow Springs soon after she had hung up the phone with Duane. However, she didn't think much of it until she arrived at the hole and lake where the alligator was spotted and then seeing the bunker where Duane had fallen. The team leader had already ordered yellow police barricade tape around the entire scene. Although there was still ample sunlight, logistics had erected lights since the sun was expected to set around 8:00 PM.

The initial scene survey had already occurred, and photographers had already taken pictures and recorded the scene. The staff at Willow Springs was very cooperative by providing video surveillance footage and player logs for the past week. Available neighboring footage was being collected. The alligator was indeed in the lake at the 4th hole. Everyone was amazed to see it so relaxed at the base of the lake, as if sunbathing.

Genie advised the team that in addition to any available DNA samples to be taken eDNA was required. eDNA is environmental genetic material created when creatures leave behind skin, scales, feces and other particles in water, soil, on land, grass and the rest of the environment. This material is used to determine the genetic makeup of various species.

Once samples from the environment are recovered, the material is put through one of several machines for testing. However, eDNA has different analysis than ordinary human DNA. Since the eDNA results would be used as part of a criminal investigation, the chief needed to make certain all procedures and testing was carried out in accordance with industry standards used for marine life.

The director of the lab had just received an invitation to attend a workshop on implementing national standards for environmental DNA (eDNA) monitoring. This was of significant interest because, at the time, the team had to send their samples to another lab to meet the stringent analytical protocols. Genie's lab, like many others across the country, faced challenges in coordination and efficiency when handling eDNA. After specimens were collected from the lake, the sample vials had to be sent to an external lab. Testing would occur to target, identify, and compare species-specific genetic markers to an online DNA database system. This process is necessary to isolate and identify the exact alligator species and determine its origin.

If the origin of the alligator could be identified and linked to the tissue removed from the child's monkey bite, it would strengthen the case against the suspected owner. The team aimed to gather as much evidence as possible to provide sufficient statistical information to support a warrant issued for the search and seizure of the suspect's home, where neighbors suspected illegal animals were being housed.

One of the pieces of evidence collected near the lake was a mud-stained bird feather. The officer used gloves to pick the feather up, labeled a specimen storage bag to be evaluated with other environmental evidence collected. Genie made a mental note of the feather especially since she knew of Duane's allergic reactions to specific bird feathers.

After the evidence was gathered from Willow Springs Golf course, the team went to the home of the child bitten by the monkey to examen the child and get statements and any evidence available.

Mrs. Jones invited members of the team into her living room. The family lived in a modest home. Mrs. Jones sat with her five-year-old son Timmy on the couch. Two evidence team members, Detective Brown and Genie, sat across from them and noticed Timmy's small bandage on his right forearm.

"Hi, Timmy. I'm Detective Brown, and this is Genie. We just want to ask you a few questions about what happened, okay?"

Timmy nodded and answered "Okay."

"Can you tell us what happened with the monkey, Timmy?" Genie asked.

Timmy fidgeting with his toy truck answered eagerly: "I was playing outside with my truck and a little monkey came over. It was nice at first. But then it took my toy and bit me when I tried to get it back.

"That sounds scary. Can you show us where it bit you?"

Timmy lifted his arm to show the bandage, "here."

Genie smiling reassuringly and said: "You're very brave, Timmy. Did the monkey look hurt or sick?"

"No, it looked okay. Just small and furry."

"I didn't see it happen, but our security camera caught everything. I have the footage here," Mrs. Jones held up a USB drive and offered it to Genie.

"Thank you, Mrs. Jones. That will be very helpful. We also have a secure link where you can upload the video directly to our portal." Detective Brown handed Mrs. Jones a card with the link.

"I'll upload it right away. I hope we've been helpful. The neighbor and I have all been commenting on the neighborhood app about the strange animal noises we've been hearing coming from the house. I think we'll finally get some answers."

"If we can identify the monkey and tie it to the neighbor's home, we'll be able to get a subpoena to search the property."

"Yeah, 'cause I want my truck back. It's the one that has the part that goes to my track."

"We'll do our best, buddy," Detective Brown said.

"Thank you both for your help."

"No problem, Mrs. Jones. Thank you for allowing our technician get a sample of little Timmy's skin from the bandage. I'm sure it'll be helpful. We'll be in touch if we need anything else."

"I'm just glad you didn't have to do any real poking to get it."

"Me too!"

"Take care, Timmy. Thanks for talking to us."

"Bye, bye!"

The team left. It had been a long day and by now everyone was complaining they were hungry.

Genie finally pulled into her driveway after a long day of investigation, her mind still buzzing with the details of the case. She unlocked the door quietly, stepping into the dimly lit living room. Duke, their loyal Rottweiler, lifted his head from his spot on the couch but quickly settled back down when he recognized her.

Tiptoeing through the house, Genie peeked into the bedroom to find Duane and Duke already fast asleep. Duane's steady breathing was a comforting rhythm that made her smile despite her exhaustion. She carefully closed the door, not wanting to disturb their peace.

In the kitchen, Genie poured herself a glass of water and leaned against the counter, her thoughts drifting back to the day's events. She was encouraged by the progress they'd made, hoping that the evidence would be enough to get what the team needed for a subpoena. The video footage from Mrs. Jones' security camera could be the key to unlocking the truth and ensuring that the suspected illegal animal owner faced justice.

Satisfied with the day's work but aware of the challenges still ahead, Genie headed to the guest room. She settled into the bed, eager for the rest she desperately needed. Tomorrow would bring new developments, and she wanted to be ready. As she closed her eyes, she felt a sense of determination wash over her. They were on the right track, and she was prepared to see it through.

For now, though, the day was done, and it was time to recharge. Genie drifted off to sleep, her thoughts already beginning to shape the next steps in their investigation.

Par For the Past

*T*wo days later Duane would find himself on the greens again. The men decided to go to Trilogy Golf course. Several of his friends, including Mike, Ricky Barry and Bobo, were enjoying a brewski at the club house after playing 18 holes at Trilogy. There was nothing short of friendly shit talking. Mike, Duane's closest friend was aware that Duane was coming out of transient amnesia and a day with the guys would be just what the doctor ordered to combat his PTSD.

Some methods of combating post-traumatic stress includes learning about the trauma and re-exposing the patient to the same or similar trauma that created the stress. The exposure confrontation should be safe stimuli in a controlled environment. Although Duane was advised to avoid alcohol, he opted to enjoy a light beer, nonetheless.

It was in late afternoon by the time the guys finished 18 holes. Everyone in the group had played basketball at one time or another, before adopting golf as the sport of choice. All the men enjoyed debating sports, and each of them exercised their skill as armchair quarterbacks and coaches from their couches. But, with golf as a growing trend, the race to keeping up with the sport and its lingo was on. After a round of golf, the fellas sat in the clubhouse watching sports, analyzing each other and once again, more friendly trash talk.

"I got more loft than I anticipated with my 9-iron today." Mike said taking a sip of beer.

"Yeah, you got a lotta loft, but you couldn't hit it straight." At six feet seven, Ricky was the giant in a group of already tall men.

"Switching over to a 3 wood really makes a difference on those longer holes. You gotta think about the distance and the wind." Duane said proudly.

"Man, distance is one thing, but I use a hybrid club to hit further. It's all about getting that extra yardage bro." The men turned and looked at Ricky with sidewise sarcasm. Several of them had whispered complaints about Rickey taking extra shots and holding up the pace of the game.

But Mike, the jokester and politician in the group, laughed it all off saying, "Ricky, man, maybe you wanna stop using some of those wooden clubs you got from the museum." The men started laughing.

"Hey, I like my wooden clubs. Gets the job done."

Duane leaned in, gesturing with his hands, "alright, fellas, let me break it down for y'all. The key is a flex shaft that's forgiving. When you swing, the club head is behind you," standing up to demonstrate. "You gotta follow through with yo swing to hit the ball. That lil whip action'll send the shit flying straight onto the greens."

Mike rolled his eyes. "Here we go, Professor Duane's golf lesson of the day."

Ricky sat down stretching his long legs while grinning. He was happy to get the heat off him. "Yeah, Duane, we know. But some of us just like to play, not overthink every shot."

All the guys chimed in "Man, shut the fuck-up. You don't know nuthin!"

Barry, who had been on the phone during the conversations looked up laughing, "I know that fool ain't talking 'bout somebody overthinking when his ass takes forever on every hole." Although the men enjoyed talking shit and clowning each other, they always did so with respect to one another. They laughed, but Ricky was serious about fine tuning his game.

"I'm telling you, it's all in the technique. Y'all knuckle heads master that, and you'll shave strokes off your game."

"Well, maybe next time I'll remember that when I'm not missing putts left and right."

"Yup, me too. True dat."

"Man, y'all notice golf is so inundated wit all that technical shit. 'Lotta AI and what not."

"Shit, my ass still getting calluses on my right hand practicing my swing."

"Y'all, look at that bullshit over there." Barry said pointing at someone walking on the golf course with a dog sitting in the golf cart.

"Is that a 'quote' *service dog?*" he asked, gesturing air quotes.

"Yeah, what the fuck's *his service*," Ricky said.

Duane shook his head in agreement. "I rather have five well behaved dogs on the greens than one human blasting Chris Brown."

"I might be ok with Snoop. Did y'all catch him carrying the Olympic torch?"

"Shiiit, my boy Snoop done broke all kinda social barriers."

"Hey, straight outta Compton."

"Man, but Snoop from 'Strong Beach.'"

"Yeah, but he grew up in Compton, Bro."

"I'm waiting to see him on the greens."

"Duke may be the only dog I know that's allowed on 'the greens.'"

"Man, there's a course over in Oceanside that let them fuckin four-legged fools all up and through there, all day long. They calling it a *'doggie caddie.'*"

"What the hell is a *doggie caddie?*"

"It's when mothafuckas have god damn dogs out on the greens."

"I saw that shit on Tiktok. Crazy. There's a whole *doggie caddie* social media group. They call it *'Yappy Hour.'*"

"I saw that too. I think it was at a course in Indian Wells.' They even giving them treats and shit."

The men ran through topics from sports to pop culture, but all trash talk came back to bolstering their golf swing.

Later that evening, after the guy's post-golf shenanigans, Duane decided to fact check a few of the guy's comments. He ended up in a rabbit hole online, researching more history about golf and golf trivia responses. Duane assumed most of the guys had no idea about the rich history of African Americans in golf —or at least they had never talked about it. Genie had suggested Duane look at the timeline of Blacks in golf as a starting point.

As Duane read various online articles about golf history, he reflected. He was surprised to read once there was a "Caucasian-only clause" in the PGA bylaws!

Duane's thoughts were interrupted by the doorbell. It was Mr. Red, Genie's father, who made a habit of stopping by unannounced. Duane, though fond and respectful of Mr. Red, nevertheless did not hold his tongue and always spoke very candidly and frank to his father-in-law.

"Red, I see you insist on ignoring my house rules, don't you?"

"Did I catch you still sleeping," Mr. Red rudely replied in true form. "I wanted to make sure you're still fit enough to take care of my daughter or if I need to pop you on your head again." He smiled as Duane stepped aside to let Mr. Red in. Mr. Red was equal in height, statue and whit as Duane and earned a living in real estate. However, unlike Duane, Mr. Red and his wife—Genie's parents—owned a large amount of residential real estate. Something Duane admired and whose success he hoped to duplicate.

When Duane was in junior high, Mr. Red allowed Duane to do his lawn and several other properties that Mr. & Mrs. Red owned in the neighborhood. From there, Duane built an enormous data base. People in the neighborhood trusted him and liked him since he was a youngster. He always made a point to stop and talk to people in the grocery store, getting gas, watering their lawn or shopping. No opportunity to meet someone new was passed by Duane.

"Any new hot listings?"

"Hey man, I didn't come here to line your pockets. Do your own research. I came to make sure you ain't crazy or something."

Duane extended his hand to Mr. Red. One of the most outstanding characteristics of Duane was his respect for elders.

"Come on in man. You want a beer or something?" Duane asked, knowing neither Mr. Red nor his wife drank.

"Yeah, nothing cheap either. Po' me yo' most expensive tequila."

"You got it man."

"Naw, I'm just kidding. So how you doing, son? Genie told me you had another one of those reactions again. What the doctors saying?"

"Man, it's enough I gotta answer to your crazy daughter. She got this dog following me everywhere. Ain't nothing happen to me."

"But this time she said you passed out. Don't say nothing happened."

"I told Genie about telling my business. Seriously man, if they can just get a read on which fuckin parasite these damn birds are carrying, the allergist says I can get shots to desensitize me against them or something like that."

"Man, you married the best person."

"I married the best woman. She ain't just a person."

"So what's going on, what cha doing now?"

The two men sat at the kitchen island. Duane drinking a fruit punch, Mr. Red taking the liberties to open the refrigerator and pour lemonade for himself.

"Several buddies of mine were debating some golf history earlier. I'm just doing a little fact checking."

Duane grabbed his laptop off the counter, opened it and showed the last page he was reading online from his computer screen.

"So, you do have a problem with your memory."

"Man, I ain't got a problem with shit. I don't know who told you that, but my mind's working fine."

"So why you gotta do...uh, what' that s you were saying, *checking fact*."

"Cause I don't believe in talking outta my ass like some mothafuckas do."

"What you saying, boy..."

"Not you, Mr. Red. I'm talking about some of these cats I hang out with. Some of my Philly boys tryna tell me Stephen A is on the 'up and up.'

"Hey, wait, I love Stephen A. He is up and up. What you don't agree with?"

"Personally, I think Stephen A is full of shit and he's been full of shit.

"What. Man, stop."

"Nah, I ain't stoppin'. Rather than supportin' someone Black, he's too busy critiquin' and puttin' us down one at a time, and that's just not cool. When his ass was on his way up the ladder, he had the support of the Black community behind him, 'cause ESPN had actually fired his ass. Then when the public begged to bring him back, and ESPN actually did, he became completely full of himself. And that's why he got his ass eaten up by them female basketball players the other week.

"Ain't no woman ever shut up Stephen A."

"You obviously ain't see what happened this time," Duane said. "These women shut him up 'cause he's had the platform to discuss women's basketball for years, and never did, but now is tryna act all holier than thou and act like he paved the way for these women in mainstream basketball conversations this year."

"Man, Imma stop you right there. Stephen ain't letting nobody shut him down."

"Man, Stephen A had nothing to say after those Black women basketball players hit him hard with: '*respectfully, with your platform, you could have been doing this three years ago, if it mattered to you!*' Man it was crickets. Mic drop. I'm glad she did, he need to be put in check."

"Speakin' of...so, you stopped playing basketball, huh?"

"I can still hoop man, but I don't want the stress on my body no more." The two men were quiet for a few moments. Like many

Black men, both enjoyed trash talking. Duane sensed Mr. Red stopped by for something else and wanted to wait to see where he was coming from.

Mr. Red reached into his top pocket and put on a pair of glasses and leaned into Duane.

"Did Genie tell you golf skills ran in our family? Look at this." Mr. Red looked away from Duane's laptop and zealously scrolled through photos on his cellular phone. "The history books leave out a lot of untold history made by people who never got any recognition. My father and his whole family were playing golf during times Black folks weren't even allowed on the court."

"The *greens*."

"What! I know what I'm talking about. Black folks weren't even allowed on *the* golf course, but the man had him carrying his bags. Humph, does that computer show the only two Black man that built and ran a golf course?!"

"Here it is," Duane said pointing to the published work on African American golf history which made reference to William Powell, an air force veteran who built a golf course."

"What were you showing me on your phone?" Duane redirected Mr. Red. Mr. Red was notorious for starting one subject and ending up on a totally different tangent. He enjoyed *controversial conversation,* yet constantly prefaced his statements with the disclaimer: '*now I don't want no controversy here…*'

Duane swiftly responded, "man, I'm listening to you. You were about to show me something on your phone about your family playing golf."

"Not just playing golf." Mr. Red said, then moved his cellphone closer to Duane to see. "Take a look here. This is my father. The first Black man allowed to even play on public golf courses in San Antonio."

Duane leaned over to look at Mr. Red's phone, but Mr. Red generously handed it to him. The article was titled: '12 Negroes On S.A. Links,' with a photo of two men over a caption that read: 'Sgt. Edward Green and Jesse Satterfield First two negro golfers to play Brackenridge golf course.'

"Wow, which one is your father."

"You tell me which one you think."

Duane looked and examined the photo closely. He had an eye for detail and correctly pointed out Mr. Red's father.

"Wow, the article says the 'city consul' had to 'pass a resolution' to even allow Blacks to play golf there."

"That's what I'm saying. And my father worked at the golf course and wasn't even allowed to play there."

"Oh, here they played at a course named the same as the one my buddy and I were at a couple days ago, 'Willow Springs.' Check this out, Blacks were limited to only being able to play at Willow Springs on "Monday and Tuesday morning only."

"Monday and Tuesdays only."

"Right!"

"That's right. And my father was good enough to work at a country club, but not good enough to play golf there! He was 'an attendant.' It took a lawsuit by the NAACP to desegregate parks and courses for golf and tennis."

"Attending to clean up after they ass but not in attendance to play there!? Wow. That would piss me off."

"Man," pointing to yet another photo of Mr. Jesse Satterfield, "pops and my whole family played golf in San Antonio, Texas. Check him out here."

"Wow, that's a good-looking man."

"Now you see where I get my looks from." Mr. Red grinning with pride.

"Musta skipped a generation and passed you up to give all the rest to Genie." Duane let out a boisterous laugh. Mr. Red snatched his phone and scrolled to show more photos and newspaper clippings of his family.

"My father taught me several important lessons that have carried me through my life. First, he's the one that taught me character is better than money. Because he worked at the clubhouse of a golf course, he use to tell me…" Mr. Red took a long pause and looked out of the window. Duane closed his laptop computer and looked directly at Mr. Red. He wanted to be sure to give Mr. Red his 100% attention. "He said players use to leave their keys, wallets, all kind of valuables man, all out in the open. On the bench when they were in the shower. The players obviously trusted each other. Maybe it was the times, or maybe they were testing each other, but he said he never had anybody complaining something was stolen. And he said they knew I was in there cleaning up, wiping down counters and everything. He said nobody tried to move or hide stuff, just open trust."

"The honor system."

"Character. A man's word. You gotta always be a man of your word."

Duane didn't want to interrupt Mr. Red. He listened intently in silence, watching and listening. There was a pause. Mr. Red's father had been married for decades but died before Mr. Red could introduce him to his wife.

Mr. Red remembered when his dad told him stories about how *his* dad—Mr. Red's granddad—spent 3 years in prison for a murder he didn't commit. "The DA had kept my grandpa in jail for 3 years. Finally removed the charges and let him go after they saw he was telling the truth. Probably why my dad wanted to instill honesty and character in us, after what happened to his dad." Duane just listened while Mr. Red continued.

"When my father came home, every night. See, he worked long, long hours, 'cause he wanted my mom to have everything. No kiddin', man, he would always have something, some kind of surprise or gift for mom. And for us too," looking up at Duane for a response, but Duane just listened. "Lotta nights he came home after we were already in bed, but he told mom to 'get 'em up.' I could hear him telling her to get us outta bed." He said proudly and giggling. "She didn't wanna wake us up, especially if it was a school night. But he wanted to see us every day. He would say to my mom, 'I haven't seen my kids all day. I got 'em ice cream' or whatever he had. No kidding man, it felt like a party when my dad came home with stuff."

"Wow."

"So, I took that lesson. Ask Genie. I try to surprise her mom like my daddy did." Mr. Red blushed and paused. "I just put like some flowers on her car seat or decorate the steering wheel with stuff before she goes to work. I usually pick a flower from our yard or some place." Laughing. "A lot of times I just pick up something I know she likes or that she mentioned she wanted. She used to eat Fritos.

Man, I would find Fritos bags everywhere. Now she's addicted to peppermints. But I do that too, man. No kidding, it's the little stuff."

Duane patiently listened to Mr. Red's monologue for over an hour. He saw love in Mr. Red eyes. He went on telling Duane about the story of how his uncle Joe introduced his parents to each other when 'Uncle Joe' was a delivery man. "Anyway man, I don't wanna go on and on, you gotta get back to work. Just think about what I'm saying."

"Nah, go on man. This is real."

"So, my mom, you know we call her Madea—"

"Everybody has one."

"Madea, you met her once before. Man, that's a beautiful woman. Before she started wearing her hair cut it was long and wavy. Kinda like Genie."

"Yup, Genie looks just like her. She said the family called her 'Mother Dear.'"

"That's what I said man. You sayin I can't speak good English? Duane just looked.

"Well, like I said. Madea use to wear it really long as a young woman. My Uncle Joe use to do deliveries to my dad's house and told dad he had a younger sister. Dad had heard about those six sisters and knew he wanted to meet the youngest. My Uncle Joe set it up. Man, I still remember my dad's face when he looked at Madea. I even remember him combing her and my sister's hair for years. You know my wife won't let me touch her head."

Duane shook his head, overwhelmed by a sudden, vivid memory of Genie. Her giggles and playful squirms whenever he touched the right side of her neck came rushing back. This flood of memories compelled him to retreat to his office as soon as Mr. Red left. He had to jump on the computer, driven by an urgent need to uncover more about Genie's grandpa. He couldn't recall if Genie had ever mentioned her grandfather playing golf, but the photo Mr. Red shared ignited a burning curiosity within him.

Legacy on the Fairway

*T*he early 50's was tumultuous. A time where African Americans were relegated to second-class citizen status and enforced racial segregation—Jim Crow, one of the most divisive decades in world history. Even children only had ½ a chance of completing high school and 1/3 a chance of completing college and entering a profession. A time when Black men were known as faithful providers, respected for their integrity, revered for their commitments, and sometimes feared for their potential retribution—embodying the essence of resilience and strength.

When a Black man called for the cavalry, they were like cowboys leading a posse, a squad, a crew—a 'self-defense party,' as courageous as superheroes, united for one cause: to rise up and seize the power of being Black—Black Power.

Duane delved online into the PGA's timeline of African American history in golf and explored the *National Museum of African American History and Culture's* online archive published by the Smithsonian. He read about how African Americans were barred from the PGA, but his quest led him deeper. Through his research, Duane discovered the untold stories of forgotten African American golf pioneers. These were the novelty players who laid the groundwork for the segregation lawsuit that Thurgood Marshall passionately argued, ultimately leading to the desegregation of golf.

Duane's heart swelled with pride and determination. The legacy of these trailblazers, including Mr. Red's father, resonated deeply with him, igniting a new sense of purpose and connection to his heritage and the game. Duane went on to read how some Whites refused to even play in and on the same parks if "Negros" were allowed to use the park. He read that in states like Virginia, *"the entire system of racial segregation was seen reeling under a mortal blow"* when a Federal Judge ruled Virginians couldn't deny Negros using of their parks. (San Antonio Register (San Antonio, Tex.), Vol. 25, No. 24, Ed. 1 Friday, July 22, 1955 - Page: 1 of 12. Magnified. The Portal to Texas History 6/13/24, 8:46 PM.)[19]

While now the term 'swatter' is used as a prank, in the 50's the term swatter was used to describe a group of golfers preparing for what was described as 'the second annual city golf tourney,' described as taking place on Nov. 3. Then he ran across an article, where Mr. Jesse Satterfield is mentioned with someone by the name "Woods," boasting of the prize money. The article placed Genie's grandfather, Jesse Satterfield, at a golf course in Willow Springs, San Antonio, Texas, with Eldridge Woods, apparently nicknamed *'Boots.'* This article published in the San Antonio Register, (San Antonio, Tex.), Vol. 23, No. 40, Ed. 1 Friday, October 30, 1953.

Duane became curious if there was any connection between this "Woods" and the golf great Tiger Woods, who coincidentally named Eldrick, prior to his nickname. But his searched didn't uncover any association between the two.

On he read. Next, he read about the PGA voting that occurred to allow Negros to participate in PGA-sponsored tournaments. Duane was overwhelmed when he read the participation was considered a "drastic change," from the Jim Crow segregation laws. Prior to the Supreme Court Ruling on desegregation there were numerous battles on the ground with local city municipalities.

Duane felt that one of his findings revealed a moment especially deserving of recognition, which was the "First Negro golfers" allowed to play golf on previously "Whites only" golf courses. These golfers are categorized as *amateur golfers*. Herein he read where Mr. Jesse Satterfield broke ground as one of two "First Negro Golfers" at Brackenridge Golf Course.

Mr. Jesse Satterfield was considered a 'local favorite,' at an annual 'state negro golf championship' at Willow Springs Golf Course in San Antonio, Texas. Duane paused for a moment, noting the coincidence that both the golf course in Texas, where Genie's grandpa played, and the city where he and Genie lived—and where he had recently played golf—shared the name *'Willow Springs.'*

"Wow." He continued reading. After the racial barriers preventing African Americans from playing golf at city parks were lifted, more articles began to surface about the newfound opportunities for Blacks to play golf. Across the nation, more and more articles were published about "firsts"—the first African Americans to play on previously segregated golf courses. "More about these trailblazers should be publicized," Duane believed. "There would be no legendary golfers today if it weren't for these pioneering players."

When many cities and states ended segregation at public parks, *The Associated Negro Press* reported comments from some municipalities, like Louisville, Kentucky, that vowed to continue it *"for some time to come, Mayor Broaddus told the delegation of NAACP members."* Many 'Jim Crow Parks' had no intention of establishing desegregation laws without a Supreme court decision. They were steadfast in their decisions were final. Duane researched for hours. He was also amused seeing advertisements for '*a dozen fresh eggs, 29¢*' and '*beef chuck roast, 44 ¢ per pound*', and '*10 lb. bag of sugar, 91¢*'.

Though Duane was determined to find articles on Genie's grandpa, he couldn't resist reading time significant articles that caught his eye. Next, he took time to read history on women in golf. He chuckled, noticing the articles referred to women as 'gals.' Then he encountered a title that read, '*Sugar Ray Favored at 13 to 10*,' by Charles Denton, Los Angeles, May 18, who characterized the boxer as '*the aging Harlem dancing master.*' Duane's eyes lit up, thinking about one of his favorite boxers, Sugar Ray Leonard, and how *Sugar Ray* could've referred to two different boxing icons, depending on the times you were in.

"Sugar Ray Robinson was a bad mothafucka. Oh, he was whooping everybody in his class. They had no answer for him. And you can tell he was sharp too!" Duane said out loud as if talking to Duke. He was fascinated to see the 1956 article. Despite the fact that the news events were well before his time, Duane had an appreciation for it. Just like he enjoyed spending time with the 'old heads' and 'OGs,' listening, talking and learning from them. The old men know a lot of history and relive those moments over and over through conversations, as if it was just yesterday.

SAN ANTONIO LIGHT 7
Tuesday, June 22, 1954

ides Claim
ns
Guatemala

[tinued from Page One]
claimed the rebels held
a in Guatemala.
TROOPS MASS
ated Press dispatches
uatemala City said Ar
oops were massing in
a of Zarapa, a city of
the main rail line be
he capital and the Carib-
y of Puerto Barrios.
flier interviewed near
dhran border said Cas-
nas men also were mov
truck towards Zarapa
the invaders headed
rail center after acti-
athedral town of Esqui-
a 5-hour battle. Three
alan soldiers were re-
killed in that engage

formed source at Tegu-
indicated a fight for
was shaping up. He
d the rebels would aban-
r guerilla tactics within
24 hours and seek a
battle with Arbenz

THER REPORTS
source also said:
least two Guatemalan
ave fled their country
ing planes since the in
began Friday.
o railroad bridges at
had been destroyed,
along the line between
and Puerto Barrios had
st; a train which left
ala City for the port ci
he has "simply disap

e rebels have taken over
town of Morales, some
from Puerto Barrios.
rebel plane machine
and dropped grenades
Jose. The rebels also
ed their planes had
Coben, a garrison town

in central Guatemala, from a
base inside the country.

BOMB THREAT
The rebel radio broadcast a
threat to bomb Guatemala City
for the fourth time since the
invasion began. The previous
three bombings were by single
planes and apparently did little
damage.
Castillo Armas has pro-
claimed his command the only
legal government of Guatemala
and called on his countrymen
to disavow the Arbenz regime.
A spokesman here said the

would announce its cabinet
later today.
Castillo Armas urged foreign
countries not to recognize en
voys of the Arbenz regime and
said he planned to send his own
representatives abroad soon.
A Cuban cabinet member, Er-
nesio de la Fe, promptly urged
his government to recognize the
rebel regime. U. S. Sen. Fer-
guson (R-Mich) said that if the
rebel forces win, he would favor U. S. recognition of the new
government.

RUSSIA

LONDON, June 22.—UP—
Moscow's newspapers joined in
a bitter new propaganda blast
today against the U. S accusing
it of touching off the fighting
in Guatemala.
Moscow radio quoted Pravda
as saying:
"No matter how U. S.
propaganda distorts the facts,
the whole world sees that the
armed attack on Guatemala
has been instigated, prepared
and carried out by the U. S.
ruling circles and (they) are
using their hirelings for this
purpose."

Cocktail Time
On Kiddies' Hour

Develops
New Tomato

FAYETTEVILLE.—UP—A
new tomato, combining the better qualities of older varieties,
has been developed by Dr. Vic-
tor M. Watts, horticulturist at
the University of Arkansas. Dr.
Watts said the tomato is strong-
ly resistant to disease and pro-
duces larger, rounder and
meatier fruit.
The new tomato is called Indark—derived from the names
of the states in which it has
been tested, Indiana and Arkansas.
Indark seeds are expected to
become available commercially
in 1955.

Eight Britons
From Red China

HONK KONG, June 22.—UP—
Two British ships arrived from
Communist China today, bringing out 8 British citizens and 36
other non-Chinese. There were
no Americans aboard.

Tempest
In Teapot

MINNEAPOLIS.—UP—
Mr. and Mrs. Martin Ross,
neighbors, seven police squad
cars, civilian defense volunteers
and a tracking dog were unable
to find Timothy Ross, 5, and
his brother, Terrence, 6, after
they left home to play. The
boys returned nonchalantly the
next morning after falling
asleep in a shed a half block
from home.

Fish Found
Trapped in Log

CHESTER, Calif.—UP—
Workmen at a sawmill cut into
a huge rotted log and out
poured about 1500 live fish
from 1 to 8 inches long. The
fish probably were trapped inside the log while it floated in
the mill pond, sawmill men
said.

Meter Promotion
For Good Will

HELENA, Mont. — UP — The
Montana Automobile Assn. has
contrived a promotional campaign designed to save motor-
ists money. A MAA representative places pennies in expired
parking meters for tardy motor-
ists. The motorist is reminded
of the good deed by a little
MAA card placed on his wind-
shield.

Reversed Truck
Leads Way to Jail

GREENVILLE, S. C.—UP—
When a man driving a truck
saw Policeman C. G. Fowler, he
threw the truck into reverse
and backed up a full city block.
The peculiar action led to investigation. The truck was
stolen. Fowler arrested the
driver.

FIRST—Sgt. Edward Green, (L), and Jesse Satterfield were first two negro golfers to play at Brackenridge Monday. The city council had passed a resolution opening city golf courses and tennis courts to
negroes Saturday. Satterfield, who shot a 78, is clubhouse attendant at Oak Hills Country club and Green,
who shot 79, is stationed at Randolph AFB. After
game, they told Course Manager Murray Brooks they
enjoyed playing and thanked him.

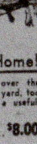

FIRST FEDERAL

SAN ANTONIO REGISTER

RIGHT · JUSTICE · PROGRESS

Links, Tennis Courts Opened, Pools Closed to Negroes

Illness of Year Claims AME's Bishop Clayborn

Negroes Get Use of Dallas City Club

Veteran, in Fight With Wife, Cop, Faces 2 Charges

City Council Passes Pool Segregation Ordinance By 5 to 2 Vote

Final Rites Held For Mother Found Dead in Bed

Death Claims Former Star San Antonio Athlete

San Antonio Hit By Week End Of Minor Violence

San Antonio Man Receives High Papal Decoration

Erring Mate's Cad "Beat Up"—but Good

Mrs. M. C. Terrell Seeks End of D.C. Hotel Jim Crow

Segregation Chief Topic of NAACP Annual Meeting

"Black Eagle" Loses His United States Passport

Hit-Run Auto Injures S. A. Man

Lawyers Guild Denies McCarthy Red Charge

Virginia Studies Ideas to Retain Jim Crow Schools

Loyalty Dismissal Of Philly Postal Employee Upheld

Honolulu Picked For Episcopalian Meet, Next Year

Woman Stabs Tardy Mate With Ice Pick

Baltimore Sup't Tells Teachers Schools to be Integrated in Fall

D. C. Youth Wins Six Scholarships Totaling $3,500

Colonel, School Board Member Gets College Degree After 50 Years

City Atty. Ruling Leave[s] Segregation Up to Council

Police Group Quell Rumors Of Break-Up

San Antonio police officers reported on the verge Wednesday of breaking up their Police Officers Assn. over handling of their latest election, closed ranks Thursday with a vote of confidence in the organization.

The vote of confidence apparently silenced all talk of forming up to as many as four different groups and junking the old organization.

In a meeting that was so harmonious even the press was allowed to stay, the police officers responded to pleas of unity from Capts. R. D. (Bob) Allen and G. E. Matheny.

Before acting they heard several officers admit they'd been considering about pulling out of the San Antonio Police Officers Assn. and forming a new one. Officers said the proposals also included a three-headed plan for forming an organization for Catholic members, one for social purposes only, a third to act as a savings and loan agency.

Forgotten at Thursday's meeting were the reports that had stirred the police force to the point of breaking up their association. In a closed session Wednesday the officers had heard a raft of charges about last week-end's election of association officers. Most dealt with handling of the ballot box by Inspector A. E. Bookout, outgoing president who becomes secretary as a result of the latest voting. Officers agreed, though, there had been no tampering.

The association officers pointed out Thursday that bylaws of the association provide for a recall if there is any dissatisfaction with leadership. Recall can be initiated by petition of 25 officers. Jack Westbrook is president-elect.

San Antonio Express

FRIDAY, JUNE 18, 1954   **c   PAGE 1 B**

Palsy Drive Fund Leader, Council Clash on Rental

The campaign chairman of Bexar County's Cerebral Palsy Assn. and drive collided with city council Thursday over an alleged $63 overcharge for municipal auditorium rental during the welfare group's $100,000 June 5-6 telethon.

After a hot exchange of words over city policies in charging auditorium rentals for charity benefits, Councilman H. J. Shearer gave Seymour Flatow, the palsy association representative, his personal check for $63. Flatow appeared before the council's regular meeting, claiming he had made a verbal contract with former auditorium manager R. D. Skiles to rent the building for $400. When he went to pay his bill after the telethon, however, Flatow complained present manager Solomon Wolf tacked on an extra $63 for cleanup fees and table rentals.

THE CAMPAIGN chairman asserted that actually he felt no rental at all should have been charged during the telethon which raised an estimated $100,000 for cerebral palsy treatment. Many show people donated their services to the 15-hour-long continuous fund appeal program, he said.

Wolf and City Manager Ralph Winton explained that auditorium rentals for charity benefits are designed to barely cover cost of operation.

Wolf then charged that dressing rooms and passageways were so littered with bottles, food, boxes, paper, and cigaret butts following the show that he was forced to hire a special crew of five men for two days to put the place back in order.

After a motion by Councilman Ralph Easley and Councilwoman

Thelma Stevens to cancel the extra $63 charge failed to carry, Shearer questioned Flatow if the city would go in care of palsied children. When Flatow assured him it would, the councilman rose dramatically to announce:

"THEN I'LL donate you the $63 so I can go to dinner. If you will go down to the city manager's office, you can pick up the check (to cancel the charge). I voted 'no' (on the motion for the city to cancel the the $63 charge)."

In the manager's office, he presented Flatow the check with a parting statement that the city could not cancel out auditorium charges for one charity without having to make it a permanent policy.

"I didn't want it this way, you know that," replied Flatow.

"That's the way you got it," snapped Winton, obviously angry.

The manager then proceeded to remind Flatow he had helped the palsy association repeatedly in preparations for the telethon and pointed out he (Winton) had refrained from telling council members of the campaign chairman's "threats" to take the $63 charge before the governing body.

Most Eligible Get Polio Shots

More than half of all eligible second-grade school children in the city have now received their Salk polio vaccinations, City Health Director George W. Rice announced Thursday.

Dr. Rice said 8,236 children, or 50.9 per cent of those eligible under the test program, have received a series of three vaccinations.

The city figure is not yet complete. Dr. Rice said, as make-up clinics are still being held.

No Action Taken On Tennis Plea

A city attorney's opinion Thursday dumped the thorny municipal segregation problem straight into the lap of city council.

The city's governing body took no immediate action, however, beyong announcing it will hold several meetings on the question in the near future.

THESE DEVELOPMENTS, or lack of them, left the segregation front virtually stalemated Thursday:

The council took no action on motions by Councilman Henry B. Gonzales to create a 15-member inter-racial commission and to open all municipal golf courses "without restriction" to Negroes.

date for the first of a series of segregation-talk meetings.

It received the opinion from City Atty. Ralph Brite, but made no immediate comment.

A NEGRO tennis group planning a tournament next week and seeking use of additional city court facilities did get the assurance of Parks Director Alvin E. Schmidt late Thursday he "will work something out for them at Woodlawn Park."

Schmidt pointed out that Negroes already have exclusive use of two courts at each of the following parks: Central Playground, Lincoln, West End, and Pittman-Sullivan. The parks director said, as far as he is concerned, Negroes can "go in and play" on Woodlawn courts when they are not in use. He suggested the same would apply to San Pedro courts, although those are more crowded.

L. E. Askey, president of the Alamo City Tennis Club, said the club wants facilities adequate to permit four matches at a time for the tournament next Thursday through Sunday. Schmidt pointed out that the San Antonio Tennis Assn has a scheduled tournament on San Pedro Courts at the same time.

Brite's opinion pointed out that the council, if it wants to continue segregation customs in use of swimming pools, golf courses, and other public park facilities, will have to pass "appropriate ordinances" under authority of state statutes.

BOTH HE and City Manager Ralph Winton contended that account of the opinion carried by

an afternoon newspaper was a "completely twisted version."

Brite did point out that there are no existing city ordinances providing segregation in parks and therefore "no legal basis upon which the administrative branch of the city government can deny Negro citizens admittance . . . if such a demand is made."

"Therefore," concluded Brite, "the question is one of policy which can only be determined by the governing body of the city, in other words, the city council."

He pointed out further that no affirmative action is necessary by the council if it wishes to drop segregation bars. In either event, however, he suggested the council "state the policy to be followed by the administrative branch of the city government in this regard."

Schmidt and Winton have made clear that no force would be brought to bar Negroes from pools or golf courses, although they will be advised not to enter.

Painter Faces Assault Charge

Arrested while at work Thursday morning, Joe E. Quiros, 33, 730 W. Harlan St., a house painter, was charged in justice court with assault to murder in the case of Juan Griego, 20, who is in a serious condition with a bullet wound in his right side.

Quiros was free on $1,000 bond on a murder charge filed against him May 3 in connection with the fatal shooting of Miguel Olivezines at Guadalupe and Nueces Sts.

Griego was found staggering along in the middle of the intersection of Loop 13 and Somerset Road early Sunday morning. Sheriff's investigator Tony Morin said the man was shot with a .38 pistol while in front of a tavern in the 700 block of Brazos Ave.

San Antonio Register (San Antonio, Tex.), Vol. 23, No. 40, Ed. 1 Friday, October 30, 1953 **Page: 5 of 12**

Tee Time Secrets

S everal days later, Duane and Genie enjoyed a rare morning of leisure hanging out in bed. Finally having a day off together was priceless. Genie had started the day with a hot cup of tea, savoring the peacefulness before climbing back into bed to join Duane. She placed the steaming cup on the bedside table, the comforting aroma filling the room. The two spooned one another, with Duane watching a women's golf tournament and Genie watching Duane. It was a rare moment of intellectual downtime for her, and she wanted to catch up with her husband after the past week. Genie knew how much Duane loved golf, but she could care less about the game. However, given Duane's last allergy attack that produced a moment of amnesia, she decided to get more connected. Three women in the LGPA were in a playoff. Genie glanced at the tournament, appreciating the women's athleticism and skill set, but also took note of their sports apparel. Some of the ladies wore pleated skirts, others straight skirts with, and some without, a split. The headgear was just as varied: some wore snazzy sunshades, others sun visors, and a couple even had someone carrying an umbrella during their stroll to the hole.

However, Duane interest was quite different.

"Honey, as a woman, I really appreciate seeing you support women sports. It's very cool of you, watching women golf." Genie said, raising up, taking a sip of tea before snuggling back in bed closer to him.

"I like watching women tournaments because of the pace they play at. It's something I can relate to as a new golfer."

"You been golfing for years now."

"But I'm still learning the game. Watching the women play helps me see how I should strike the ball based on how I'm standing, my balance, and the terrain of the course. All those little things make a difference. It's not just coming out and hitting the ball up and down the course. Watching the women really teaches me how to have a better flow and a better level of patience with myself, as well as how the game should be played."

"Aww. Honey, that's so sweet hearing you say you want to have patience with yourself. So humble and modest of you." Genie blushed, taking yet another sip of her hot tea, feeling a warm glow from Duane's words that was as soothing as the tea. "How do you compare a woman's game to the men?"

"Actually, the women's game is lot easier for a new golfer. Someone new to the sport can pick up technical skills watching women's golf because it's closer to how you're going to play. Of course, I'll never play at the level these women play in the tournaments. But the pace that the women play and how deliberate they are with their putting stroke is good to watch and learn versus how some of the men putt and their driver shots.

"Hmm, well men, all things being equal, pound for pound, are obviously stronger than women. I get it."

"A lot of men play by taking their driver out and blasting the ball down the fairway. I'm not gonna blast the ball 300 something yards." Duane said humbly. "Well, occasionally I might try, but not on a regular basis. Maybe every blue moon or somethin'. But the accuracy that women play with is refreshing for someone like me who's new to the game. I can relate better to the professional women's game than the professional men's game."

"Do the women play the same course as the men?"

"Of course. Women play the same number of holes too. But they don't play the same distance. The tee boxes are set up a little different because of the strength of most men." Duane elaborated, "look, when women step to the tee box they may not tee off as far as the men, but women are way more accurate. By comparisons, a man'll get up and swing hard and blast the ball 'cause their nuts are in the way, but the women'll hit the ball more accurately." Men have a lot of power to hit the ball further down the fairways, but in the women have a better pace in their game.

Genie snickered and sat up on her husband's shoulder for a better view.

"Ok see Genie, babe, watch for a second. See, these three women are all tied at the end of the tournament. Now they're getting ready to tee off again for a playoff, to see who breaks the tie."

"Oh, ok. That's interesting."

"Now, these three women have to play the 18th hole over again to break the tie. They're gonna tee off now."

Genie noticed two cherry red square boxes standing out against the lush green grass. "Oh, so they have to stand between those two square boxes?"

"Ok, that's the actual 'tee box.'"

"It's like two cherries," Genie said flirting. "Hmm, why haven't I ever seen those bright red boxes on the golf course before. Is it because they're in a playoff?"

"It's 'cause you never pay attention. Those tee boxes are at the beginning of each hole. Remember, I told you before, they're color-coded. They may not always be square boxes, sometimes the tee boxes are painted on pieces of wood."

Genie directed her attention away from Duane's muscular back and watched each of the three women step up to the tee box. Despite their different statures, Genie appreciated their athletic skills. The arm motion, swing rotation, and ability to focus and balance were incredible. Given her love for theatre, Genie also appreciated the commentators' real-time broadcasting skills and admired their choice of words.

"On the bag? What does that mean honey?"

"That's the caddie. That player's caddie's her dad."

"Oh, that's so cute. They're carrying the golf bags for the women." Genie blushed sarcastically. "Would you carry my bags," kissing Duane on the neck and shoulder. He rolled into Genie's direction, putting his legs between her's.

She said in a sensual tone, "the golf sticks have covers on their heads," gushing. "Why is that? To keep them warm?"

"No babe, that's not to keep the golf heads warm, licking Genie's ear. "The covers on the golf heads are to keep the clubs from making so much clanking noise."

"We don't need any covers on the head, do we?"

"Naah. It's better without the covers. And you can make all the noise you want." Duane flipped Genie on top of him. "Also, it's good to have, so the club heads don't get chipped." Genie's breasts dangled over Duane's lips. "And the covers keep the clubs clean too."

"Oh, do they? Well, I like it real messy."

"Don't forget, when a person takes a whack, dirt and grass can get stuck on the head." Genie's eyes got larger. She knew a position on top of her husband was danger in the moment. She flipped herself back over. She wanted to learn from the game and wanted to avoid arousing her husband anymore.

"Well, let me check out this tournament." She said teasing Duane.

The couple redirected their attention back to the tournament. The three players each struck the balls down the fairway with remarkable accuracy. As one player's ball landed, the announcer made an early prediction, calling the player's ball "catching too much speed going down" and missing the green, landing in the fringe. Meanwhile, the last player's ball landed in a bunker. Seeing the player go into the bunker gave Genie a moment of anguish as she reflected on her husband's allergic reaction.

"Oh no! It landed in a bunker."

"It's ok. This girl's clutch. Watch, she can still putt for eagle on this shot and win the tournament," Duane said calmly. The player showcased her remarkable fearless skill without hesitation, took a strong solid stand and appeared to simply flick the ball out of the sand to roll onto the greens. The crowd oohed. She was the last of the three to take a shot onto the greens.

"Nice!" Genie praised the golfer's skill.

"Ok, she didn't put the ball in the hole, so now each woman takes a shot on the green again for the hole to score a birdie. They're on the 18th hole."

"What if they all three put it in the hole."

"Then a three-way playoff is forced again, but they go to the 17th hole." Each woman scored a birdie again. The suspense during each shot was evident to Genie. She started paying closer attention.

"Ok, see babe. Since they made it all three go to the 17th hole to see if the tie can be broken for a win."

"Oh, so they're working backwards on the course now?"

"Exactly."

A golf cart carried the three women to the 17th hole. Duane explained that during a tiebreak playoff, players are driven to the hole instead of the usual walking during a tournament. This way, TV time is spent more on the moment of suspense rather than logistics.

Genie noted various product logos on practically everything. The women all went up to the 17th hole and teed off once more on a three-shot hole. Each woman took their time to note the challenge the fairway presented, then a loud 'ting' with their strikes, and each ball floated down the lush fairway. While announcers assessed the women's tee-off, the analytics of their strikes to landing appeared on the screen. Genie, with her expertise in DNA and forensics, found the tournament increasingly interesting.

The player whose ball lands furthest away from the cup is allowed to strike first in rotation to attempt an eagle. If one player scores an eagle, and the other two players only birdie, the player who scores an eagle wins. However, if two golfers only par and one golfer scores a birdie the player who scored a birdie wins. If two players score a bogey and one player scores a par, the one who scores a par finally wins the tiebreak.

The announcers commented on the pressure the women were under during their strokes. The remaining two women each took a shot but failed to put the ball in the hole, requiring a third shot. While the remaining two women scored a par, it wasn't good enough to beat the player who scored a birdie, thus the player who shot a birdie would win the three way tiebreak and thus win the entire tournament.

If two made a birdie, then a two-way playoff would commence in the same manner.

"Wind is coming from the left. A tree is blocking her view," one announcer pointed out in a quiet tone.

"If she can '*hit a low heater*' for birdie, she'll put pressure on the others," the second announcer whispered.

"This is basically the ultimate game of chicken," Duane smized.

"Honey, what makes a person a good putter?"

"They put the shit in the hole like this woman usually does.

Watch, she's always solid." Duane's prediction was accurate. The largest of the three women was indeed 'solid coming down the stretch,' as Duane predicted. She scored on her second shot to make a birdie. Now the other two golfers were apparently under enormous stress because a miss requiring a third shot would only make par and result in a loss to the player who scored a birdie. Since one player already scored better than par, the other players would lose by only shotting the ball in the hole on par.

All eyes were on the other two women to score a birdie to see if yet a 3rd three-way tie would be forced, or a two-way tie to avoid a loss on the 17th hole. The remaining two women each took a shot but failed to put it in the hole and required third shots. While the remaining two shot on par, it was not good enough to beat the woman who scored better with a birdie, thus winning the entire tournament.

"Wow, I get it now," Genie shouted.

Duane, happy to see his wife excited, leaned in closer to Genie, his large, luscious lips—a hallmark of his handsome features—meeting hers in a kiss so passionate it made her heart race, her body throbbed. His mahogany skin, warm and inviting, felt like a comforting embrace against her. Genie could feel herself melting, her body responding instinctively to the intense connection between them. Genie gripped the sheets and arched her back as far as she could to take as much as she were able of her husband. She surrendered to the moment, relaxing her body, feeling as if she were dissolving like hot butter under the heat of his kiss, and full of all she could take in of her husband's strong, thick, bar of love. Their love and desire intermingling and creating an undeniable spark.

Duane tenderly took his time with Genie. Each stroke as patient and slow, careful not to force more than she could handle. He cradled her hips, cupped her round butt between his hands and the firm bed, he arranged her gently to accommodate his passion, watching her expression and loving her courage. Ravishing Genie easily to full delight and complete exhaustion, Duane waited till Genie's passion was fulfilled. Her hair, soft skin, and thighs drenched in 'an ocean of love,' resonant of Genie's poetry in motion. Genie and Duane's love reached the next level.

"Babe, I'm learning you're not always a grizzle bear," Genie said returning after a quick shower. "You can actually, really be a real teddy bear sometimes. There's a certain gentle humbleness about you that's so cute," gingerly rolling back into bed. "When we were in high school, I always thought you were so cocky. I thought you were so mannish. I really didn't like you. Sometimes even when I hear you talk with the guys, it sounds like you're so cocky with all the trash talk."

"Babe, I think it's not for everyone to see this side of me!"

Genie smiled was a smirk. "Well, I'm glad I get it."

"Yeah. Some things are just for you, babe. Nowadays people don't get that…everything ain't intended for everybody. People can't tell what to keep to themselves. Too much posting real shit on social media."

"Definitely, very true."

"Like remember when your niece was going through all that years ago and she was telling us about it, then I saw her posting about it on social media too. She didn't get it then and I don't think she'll ever get it."

"Yeah, Darla does kinda do too much online. Sometimes she need to just log off and put the phone down."

"Exactly! I remember somethin' she posted on Facebook that had the whole family talking. I tried to give her some wisdom that she may not realize who's watching that may have bad intentions—because you know I've learned my lessons with this social media. Too many times, I've seen people would rather watch you crash and burn or abuse what they know about you than help you. I don't think she was hearin' me, though." Genie listened and snuggled back up to Duane.

"Speaking of…I think I'm ready to know why ladies called you 'Mr. Goodbar.' Let's get into that." Genie said with a giggle. For many years she avoided asking or digging into the topic, because she didn't really want to know. The last thing she wanted was to hear about some other woman or women with the man she's fallen in love with.

"Baby, it was always just a stage name. Simple as that."

"But that name really took off! So many people knew about you for it. To this day, we can't go nowhere without someone recognizing you know. You had quite a *reputation*. Beyond high school, you really know so many people. I always knew you were popular, but the ladies love Mr. Goodbar."

Duane took a deep breath and paused before answering.

"Honey, all that happened way before you and I got together. So, why does it matter?"

"I'm just curious, that's all. Aren't I allowed to be curious about it? I'm intrigued... Of course, I'll always know you from before that name, but it's like a whole phase of our lives that we lived completely separate and out of touch. Wouldn't you be curious if I had a fun, sexy alias. Besides, I know you for who you are now regardless of what you *may* have been before. I love you for the honest, man of integrity that I married. That's unshakable. So, what's the big deal? Were you a player?" Duane was silent. "Duane," Genie insisted jokingly, "were you a player...collecting baddies like infinity stones?"

Duane looked into Genie's eyes with a boyish smirk and responded with emphasis, "hell yeah," then grinned.

"Well, I guess you've never been modest, huh?" Genie shook her head.

"Modesty is for people with low self-esteem, I ain't the one."

"Oh lord, that's what I get for asking. Now, you gonna tell me how folks came up with the name Mr. Goodbar?"

Duane sighed. "Ok. Well, I used the name because I used to be an exotic dancer. You knew this already. Even both of my parents knew when I started. I needed to raise money for tuition. I know you can't relate to that, Ms. Smarty. While you got a full academic scholarship, I didn't."

"But I thought you got a football scholarship, didn't you?"

"Yeah, I played football for State University, but I didn't get nearly enough from that to cover tuition, books, and housing.

Genie shook her head acknowledging.

"I needed to raise money for school. I competed in some body building contests, won a few, got a little money. Kinda built a reputation for this body, then fell into exotic dancing. The demand was there, and the pay was great—just what I needed for school. Mr. Goodbar was just a stage name I made up."

"But honey, that's my question…how did you," opening her eyes wide pausing for a moment, "or if it wasn't you, who came up with it? Did some woman or women give you the name?"

"No babe. Actually, I came up with the idea myself. Just lookin' like a good bar of chocolate. Don't you agree? I know it seems too simple for you to believe. but I'm a man; it's not that deep and don't need to be complicated. It was obviously catchy and to the point, and it just stuck. That's how you know it's good…like Mr. Goodbar, himself."

Genie chuckled.

"See, I can play on words just like you babe. It may not be as poetic, but I can be creative."

Genie still wasn't convinced that was all. She knew there had to be more to the name given the enormous size of Duane's penis. Duane paused again trying to avoid going deeper into the conversation.

"Mr. Goodbar. Mr. Goodbar," Duane said shaking his head. "Baby, there's a Mr. Goodbar that was actually...a psychopathic killer and he used to abuse the shit out of women. That's who Mr. Goodbar really was." He tapped Genie playfully on the nose. Her eyes widened with shock and disbelief.

"You never heard of that movie?"

"Are you serious? Of course not! I didn't see the movie. I never watched saw *Saving Private Ryan*, or *Blood Diamonds,* or even *Shaft*—I hate movies about people killing people!"

"That's so unbelievable, considering your line of work."

"In real life, I don't like to see people or animals get killed either! I'm not in the business of hurting, I'm on the side of helping."

"Life imitates art right."

"Hopefully not here."

Duane ticked Genie playfully, then kissed her softly.

"Well, I have called myself a chocolate pack full of nuts. That's all. It's not like the movie was made for me. I would not have picked out the symbolism between a killer and myself. I just thought about a candy bar."

Genie shook her head in disgust. "I never knew that there was fuckin' movie about a killer named Mr. Goodbar! Damn."

"Listen, I found out about this after the fact. I'm just a curious mind and discovered this from back in the 70s. See, I listen to people of all ages, read and watch stuff from before my time, just out of curiosity. It was from a movie that Mario van Peebles made. And the movie was actually filmed in LA. The character got into it with the cops and he was on the run. You should look it up. He fucked a whole group of women. I mean a gang of women; they were all white chicks, but he fucked them all at the same time."

"What do you mean, at the same time. All at once?"

"Yeah, it was wild, and had some moments that were kinda dumb and unserious, you know what I'm sayin? But it was one of the classics in my eyes and Mario van Peebles is a legend for it. It never got real popular in the US, but the movie did well overseas. I guess, the contents didn't take well over here. But I think overseas it really blew the fuck up. I believe even won an award for it overseas, too. It kinda made him look like a quack out here, though. He wasn't a quack, he was ahead of himself—ahead of the times."

Genie shook her head in shock. "Oh, lord."

"Well, all kinds of stuff is out there baby. You live and work in a bubble. It's out there. I just took the name and played off the candy bar idea. The movie was a coincidence."

"Now, how 'bout you tell me, in true Genie fashion, how you got in the arms of Mr. Goodbar?"

"Are you asking me to do one of my dramatic readings?"

"Babe, however you gotta do it."

Genie wrapped herself up in sheets, tucking the top in for an off-shoulder look, leaving her legs free to straddle Duane. He grinned knowing his wife was about to give him a special private performance.

"The Snow Picture," looking squarely into Duane's tight, almond-shaped eyes that were even more narrowed by his broad, joyous smile.

"Ok, take me there, girl." Duane sat lay sturdy and attentive.

"I pictured on some foggy day
The first month of this year.

Three days I've been requesting.
Though I thought would never get here." Genie
became animated, looking up in the ceiling.

"I pictured a drive to the northern end
Where all my fantastic dreams begin
With scenic curves so soft each turn
The higher we climbed, the more we'd yearn

I pictured our conversation
Would be at great length
Exchanging the experiences that life had sent
Time would be still
As we crept each hill
I pictured you'd find the way

To the resort in my mind appear snow
A state I'd come to know
A sensation I long to exist
And with you I dare not resist," Duane blushed.
Genie's rose higher on her knees.

"I pictured I'd show you my trust
And confidence that's *way* deep inside
And during our climax at love in the snow
My passion would not creep and hide," she giggled.

"I pictured your smile of achievement
Cause you knew it would last the way home
And the next time we would lay eyes
The snow picture would have shown." Her eyes were bright.

Duane's proud smile said it all. He kissed Genie passionately.

"That's beautiful baby. So when you right that?"

Genie shrugged her shoulders.

"Come on, one more. One more. One for your Mr. Goodbar. I wanna hear more about that 'passion deep inside.'"

Genie blushed and didn't hesitate complying. She appreciated her husband as a one-man audience.

"I'll call this one, '*Mr. Goodbar's Flame.*'"

"Ohh, I like that. Lay it on me girl."

"He's warm enough to melt

Can even taste the flavor

His very scent, is one to savor.

Mr. Goodbar's candy fills my space

Till his love and my heart's encased

The moon seems to glow in the dark

His smile lights up the night

We're two candles burning with passion and heating

One flame when the fire is hot!"

The world around them fading away as Duane's strong arms encircled Genie, drawing her even closer. The intensity of their connection left her breathless, her senses overwhelmed by the feel of his mahogany skin against her own. Just as she felt herself slipping further into the blissful embrace again, a shrill ringtone cut through the air.

Genie groaned in frustration, not wanting the moment to end.

"Ugh, of course," she muttered, reluctantly breaking away from Duane's lips. "Where is it?" she said, searching through the tangled covers.

Duane, still holding her gently, chuckled softly. "Go ahead, babe. It might be important."

She finally found the phone wedged between the pillows and glanced at the screen, seeing a familiar number from work. "It's someone from the lab," she sighed, knowing she couldn't ignore the call.

"Better answer it," Duane encouraged, giving her a supportive smile even though he, too, was disappointed by the interruption.

Genie took a deep breath and pressed the answer button, her voice still tinged with the warmth of their moment. "Hello, this is Genie," she said, trying to mask her reluctance with professionalism. It was one of the detectives calling Genie informing her the evidence gathered had created a match. Genie jumped up running to her computer with excitement and opened her data base noting eDNA results populating.

"You've got enough for a search warrant," Genie replied.

"Indeed, and we'll need you to join us when you go in," officer Prader said. Genie's fist pump made Duane smile with pride. The team would be able to search the suspect's home believed to house illegal exotic animals. The monkey had apparently escaped. How the alligator's presence came to be at Willow Springs was unexplained, the eDNA confirmed the monkey's and alligator's paths had crossed. Other eDNA gathered in the suspect's neighborhood was tied to the suspect's home.

Bonds Beyond the Course

*I*t was Duane's first time in a year playing golf without his service dog, Duke. Having gone through a series of allergy shots to build immunity against the mites causing his reactions, Duane's doctors confirmed he had developed enough resistance to avoid emergencies. He convinced Genie that carrying pills was sufficient for his needs now, and although he loved Duke, having the dog with him everywhere was far from Duane's personality, despite support from his friends who had become accustomed to having Duke around—some even attached.

Duane and his friends were at Pelican Hill Golf Course, teeing off early in the morning. Pelican Hill has a stunning backdrop of the Pacific Ocean. The fairways were shrouded in thick drizzle and pockets of poor visibility in the distance. The greens were already moist from early morning dew, and some areas were slightly muddy. A storm cloud overhead continued to hover, releasing a continuous stream of thick drizzle, adding weight to every blade of grass.

Making matters worse, the group ahead of Duane and his friends ignored basic golf etiquette and courtesy. The men whined on every shot and loudly analyzed every missed putt, each one seemingly double-bogeying. Duane and his friends had hoped for a relaxing day on the greens, but the day dragged on with a thick breeze lifting balls unpredictably. Despite adjusting their irons, the balls followed the whims of the weather.

"I can deal with the environment, but playing behind these cats is the kicker," Billy Ray said, frustration evident in his voice.

"This is one time I wish a storm cloud would just dump water on the grass. Maybe these mothafuckas would just drive off in the cart and get the hell outta here," Mike added, shaking his head.

Every hole took three times longer because of the group ahead of them, and the guys were irritated.

"My whole rhythm is fucked up," Shelby grumbled, scuffing the ground with his shoe.

Duane stayed quiet, focused on his shots. Despite the conditions and the slow pace, he remained calm and patient. His phone buzzed, and he saw it was Genie calling from her conference in Austin, Texas.

"Hey, babe," Duane whispered, trying not to disturb his friends. "What's up, you good?"

"Duane! I just visited Brackenridge Golf Course! You know, the one where Grandpa was featured in the newspaper?" Genie was talking so loud Duane turned the volume down on the phone. Her excitement was palpable.

"Ok, ok. Cool, that's great" Duane walked away from the group and replied softly listening to her story while keeping an eye on his friends who were preparing to putt.

"You should see it, Duane. I can't believe it. The history, the atmosphere… It's incredible. I'm so excited. I wanted to see if I can get in touch with their marketing director to tell him who I am."

"Don't be surprised if they don't know who you are, babe. That was so long ago, you know."

"Well, yeah, but I had sent an email already and…"

"Babe, I don't mean to cut you off," whispering, "but I'm out here with Shelby, and the guys."

"Oh, you're playing golf now? How's the weather?"

"Um, babe, it's all good. Miss you too, but let me hear all about it when you get home." Pausing. "And I'm fine without Duke. I left him at home."

Duane promised again he would get back to her, but Genie kept talking. Realizing how excited she was, Duane went ahead and listened patiently to everything else she had to say, whispering short responses.

Despite the challenges of the day, Duane felt at peace. He wasn't irritated like his friends, choosing instead to enjoy the moment and the game. The day had turned into a bust, but he was content, appreciating the progress he had made in his health and the time he's spending with his closest friends.

As they approached another frustratingly slow hole, Bill muttered, "Man, if they don't pick up the fuckin' pace, I might just stick a pin in my eye."

Mike nodded in agreement, "I feel you, man. This is ridiculous. We could've been on another round by now."

Shelby sighed, "I just want one clean shot without having to wait ten minutes."

Duane chuckled, "Patience, guys. We're here to enjoy the game, remember?"

"Who can enjoy this?" Bill rolled his eyes, "Easier said than done, Duane. You're too calm for this mess. What'd you take before you got here. I want some of what you on."

"Yeah, pass it to me, too," Mike chimed in. He was usually one of the calmest between the four, but even Mike was irritated.

Duane smiled, "Just trying to make the best of it. Since that last big reaction, I've learned to not sweat the small stuff. Just ain't worth it. I don't deal with the bullshit anymore."

The men all noticed Duane's resolve and gave him kudos.

Later, as they finally finished the 18th hole, Mike threw his hands up, "Finally! Thought we'd never make it."

Bill grinned, "Next time, we book a private course. No more of this nonsense."

Shelby laughed, "Agreed. But hey, at least we made it through without a meltdown."

Duane nodded, feeling a sense of accomplishment despite the challenging day. The four decided to pass on the usual drinks afterwards since they had lost so much time already. As they packed up their gear, Duane looked forward to the next adventures, knowing that no matter the obstacles, he could handle them with patience and resilience. Although he missed Duke's company riding home, he was happy to see Duke greet him at the door when he arrived home.

Several days after the frustrating golf game with his friends, and grueling financial transactions that finally closed, Duane found himself at home on a relaxing Sunday with Genie doing her thing as usual. The morning sunlight filtered through the family room windows as he lounged on the leather couch, remote in hand, flipping between channels—the latest golf tournament and Sunday football. The soft murmur of both sports' commentary mixed with occasional applause of fans on the golf channel, and crowd roars on football channels filled the room, providing a soothing background to the day.

Genie, recently returned from her conference in Austin, Texas, sat at the dining table with her laptop open, papers strewn around her. She was deep in thought, her fingers occasionally pausing over the keyboard as she processed the information before her. Despite the calm atmosphere, Genie was feeling slightly off. Her stomach had been bothering her since she got back, but she chalked it up to her irritable bowel syndrome, a familiar nuisance that she had learned to manage over the years.

He noticed Genie's discomfort and offered occasional words of comfort and encouragement between nodding off and watching the games. He wanted to give Genie as much support as he could because he loved her and had learned to be patient with her numerous stomach issues. His gentle reassurances and quiet presence were a testament to the deep bond they shared, even in the midst of their everyday struggles.

"Hey Duane," Genie called out, looking up from her laptop. "I forgot to tell you…"

Duane muted the TV and turned his full attention to her, his eyes soft with concern and interest. "Tell me what? What's up, babe?"

"The case involving the alligator and the boy bitten by the monkey. They finally reached a verdict Friday. The jury found several men guilty of housing illegal animals."

Duane's eyebrows raised in surprise. "Yup, you knew it. Same thing happened as that Reggie alligator case years ago. That's great news. All your hard work paid off. I bet your team is happy that one is over."

"Yup," Genie said, a hint of pride in her voice. "The eDNA I identified was crucial in the trial. It helped convict those men."

Duane smiled warmly. "You're getting good at this. I always knew your work was important. I'm proud of you, Genie."

"And you know what else?" Genie continued, her eyes brightening. "Remember that white feather we found on the golf course? It proved to be one of the key pieces of evidence used at trial.

"That's the one from the illegal birds they were keeping?

"Yup. From the same species tied to your allergies."

Duane smiled, shaking his head in agreement. "Well, that explains a lot. I'm glad we got to the bottom of it."

"Like the Word says. *All things work together for the good.*" She smiled, feeling a sense of accomplishment and relief. Being able to help her husband, once again, was yet another affirmation she married the right man. Despite her stomach issues, the support from Duane made her feel better. She got up from the table, walked over to the couch, and sat beside him. Duane wrapped an arm around her, pulling her close.

"You're amazing, you know that?" Duane said softly.

Genie leaned her head on his shoulder, feeling the warmth of his embrace. "I couldn't have done it without you," she replied.

As they sat together, the soft murmur of the TV continued in the background, the day's events gradually fading away, leaving only the comforting presence of each other.

"Oh, and there's something else," Genie added, her tone becoming a bit more hesitant. "I ran into Alan at the court in the hallways, after the verdict was announced."

Duane's attention peaked, his curiosity and a hint of pride evident. "Oh really? And how did that encounter go?"

"His firm was there on another one of their traffic cases and of course Alan was there but not as a lead attorney," Genie snickered and continued, pausing to take a deep breath as a wave of nausea hit her. She pressed a hand to her stomach, waiting for it to pass before continuing. "You know how he exaggerates everything, but I knew the truth."

Duane couldn't help but gloat a little, a smirk forming on his lips. "I could always tell you weren't feeling Alan, from the second I saw you two at the bar. So, how did he take the news of your success?"

Genie smiled weakly, still feeling a bit queasy. "He heard about the verdict, and tried to play it cool, but I could tell he was a little jelly," Genie smirked. "Um, it felt kinda good, though, knowing that my work had made such a difference in getting a verdict. You know he always tried to undervalue me as an analyst. He always had to reference the fact that I not an attorney and he is."

Duane chuckled; his pride evident. "Well, you deserve all the recognition, babe. Come here." Genie snuggled on the couch with Duane. "Alan's just a footnote in your story now." Duane kissed her neck.

"In our story."

Duane nodded and kissed her again, rubbing the back of her hair with admiration.

Genie blushed softly, despite her discomfort. "Period."

They shared a moment of silent understanding, their bond stronger than ever. Duane rubbed her back as if she were a lucky charm, offering comfort and support. "That's my babe. Never forget that."

Genie pooched her buttock into him, a little more in fetal position to soothe her stomach and nestle herself against her loving man. She was grateful for his unwavering support. "So sweet. Thanks, baby. I couldn't have done it without you." She turned to face him, pressing her breasts against Duane's bare chest, and kissed his lips, savoring their fullness as if indulging in her favorite, delicious ice cream cone.

The soft murmur of the TV continued in the background, blending with the warmth and love that filled the room. Despite the challenges and discomfort, they found solace in each other's presence. Duke sensed the moment of love between the couple and honed in on the moment, nudging his wet nose between the two. The little puppy Genie once hugged on the couch was now too big to fit.

"Duke." Genie said dragging out his name.

"Uh huh, see what you did. Now you got him all excited."

Genie rolled her eyes as both of them struggled to detach their oversize pup, but Duke was not having it. He wanted the love too and Duane and Genie conceded a slither of space.

"Big baby."

"Who's the baby, you or him?"

Genie had another turn in her stomach and cuddled into Duane finding a comfortable spot for the rest of the day. In the quiet aftermath of their conversation, as the final echoes of the sports' post-game show and analysis faded from the screen, Duane and Genie lay intertwined, their hearts and minds closer than ever, having uncovered new layers of understanding and love. Genie was forever thankful to Duane for opening her eyes to the legacy her grandpa left behind.

Satterfield's Legacy Remembered

G enie, short for Regina, was a name bestowed upon her by her parents, a nod to her father Reginald. The name Genie in this story is a pet name given to the ghost author of this book by her parents, as her father's name is Reginald. The accountings of Mr. Jesse Satterfield are true as he is the real-life grandfather of the ghost author. All accountings of Mr. Jesse Satterfield are true and accurate based on family stories and newspaper clippings depicted.

While the story of Duane's Tee Time Adventures is fiction and set in contemporary times, the roots of the characters run deep into the rich soil of history. Duane and Genie, portrayed as a couple in their mid to late thirties, are in grounded in reality and both are proud descendants of fourth and fifth-generation African Americans born free from the bonds of slavery.

Genie's grandfather, Mr. Jesse Satterfield, is the true subject of this epilogue, dedication and backdrop of this story. His life story, a blend of family lore and historical records, is a testament to resilience and the pursuit of dignity in the face of systemic racism.

Born and raised in San Antonio, Texas, Mr. Jesse Satterfield was a man of integrity and honor. He married into a large, close-knit family, becoming the father of four children. Jesse worked long hours as a locker room attendant at Willow Springs Golf Course, a job that, while humble, was a pillar of support for his family. Despite the grueling hours, he always made time for his children, bringing home treats like ice cream and insisting on seeing them, even if it meant waking them from their sleep. This small but significant gesture underscored his deep love and commitment to his family.

Jesse's reputation at the golf course was admired and recorded. Members of the club trusted him implicitly, often leaving their personal belongings in his care without hesitation. This level of trust was particularly remarkable given the racial prejudices continuing through the late 1940s and early 1950s and beyond. These were the years before the Professional Golfers' Association (PGA) allowed African Americans to compete—a change that wouldn't come until the landmark decision in 1952, as reported by the *Galveston Daily News*. This decision was described as "drastic," underscoring the significant barrier it represented at the time.

During Jesse's lifetime, African Americans faced severe restrictions in education and every aspect of life, including simple recreational activities—as in accessing municipal golf courses across America and throughout Texas due to segregation laws. These laws restricted "Negros" to play golf only two days a week, relegating their access to city-owned facilities like parks, swimming pools, and golf courses to specific times.

Prior to the Supreme Court decision in the landmark case of *Brown v. Board* argued by Thurgood Marshall, history records in newspaper that African Americans playing in golf tournaments were segregated and only allowed to play on certain days. In 1948, the San Antonio Light reported on a golf tournament in which as many as 70 African American golfers participated, with Jesse was noted as a "leading contender for the title." Jesse Satterfield's name appeared in several local newspapers, including the *San Antonio Light* on July 7, 1953, which referenced "Negro golf championships occurring at Willow Springs Golf course." This was during the same years that Eldridge Woods played golf, and when Lee Elder, who later became the first African American to play in The Masters, was also active.

Jesse Satterfield's name appeared frequently in local newspapers, celebrating his achievements and resilience in the face of systemic exclusion. Jesse Satterfield's presence on the golf course during these years marked him as one of many pioneers alongside figures like a golfer named Eldridge Woods and Lee Elder, who went on to become the first African American to play in The Masters.

Citizens in San Antonio quickly mobilized for the desegregation of golf courses. Petitioners gathered 97 signatures to present to the mayor, demanding access to municipal golf courses. Following the resolution, Jesse Satterfield and Sgt. E. Green were featured as "the first two negro golfers to play at Brackenridge." Jesse had a good day of golf, shooting a 78, and Green shot a 79. Their photos later appeared in the *San Antonio Light* and San Antonio Register a week later [16, 17].

In 1954, a year marked by significant social and technological shifts, Jesse Satterfield emerged as a trailblazer, becoming one of the first African Americans to play golf at Brackenridge Park Golf Course in San Antonio. This historic milestone occurred against a backdrop of remarkable developments and transformations in American life.

The fascination with telephones was burgeoning, with newspapers highlighting the novelty of daily phone diaries and the affordability of calls, which Southwestern Bell advertised as costing "pennies a call." This was a time when the prices of everyday items were almost unthinkable by today's standards: a can of pork and beans and Kleenex cost ten cents each, a pound of steak was sixty-nine cents, and twelve bottles of Coca-Cola were just thirty-six cents. Texas, still deeply invested in cotton production, transported this vital crop via railways. The plant was still considered one of the most useful plants in the world. People were encouraged to use railways over cars. During this era, more people owned transistor radios than televisions, and Walt Disney introduced his first television show, "Disneyland."

The year began with the Rose Parade being broadcast in color, although only fifty percent of movies were made in color at that time. In sports, legendary African American baseball player Willie Mays made his iconic over-the-shoulder catch, contributing to the Giants' World Series win. Despite this achievement, African Americans represented only 7% of players in Major League Baseball and were seldom represented in broader white America.

In the world of entertainment, the number one movie was "*White Christmas*," a testament to the fact that half of all films were still produced in black and white. The top rock and roll song was "*Shake Rattle and Roll*," and Elvis Presley was rising as the "*King of Rock and Roll*." B.B. King's "*You Upset Me Baby*" was the year's biggest R&B hit. Meanwhile, Doris Day's song from "*Calamity Jane*" won an Academy Award, and "*A Star is Born*" received five Oscar nominations, although "*On the Waterfront*" took home the Best Picture award. The Academy Awards celebrated its 25th year with William Holden winning Best Actor for "*Stalag 17*," triumphing over Marlon Brando, Richard Burton, Montgomery Clift, and Burt Lancaster. Audrey Hepburn won Best Actress for her role in "*Roman Holiday*," and the Best Motion Picture award went to "*From Here to Eternity*."

Hattie McDaniel had made history in 1940 as the first African American ever to win an Academy Award. It would be her supporting role in "*Gone with the Wind*," that made history, but it would be another twelve years before Sidney Poitier would become the first African American to win a Best Actor Oscar for his role in the movie "*Lilies of the Field*," which won at the Academy's 36th annual awards highlighting nonetheless that African Americans were rarely represented in white America.

However, 1954 was perhaps most profoundly remembered for the mass vaccination of children against polio, a significant public health achievement. This context of progress and evolving societal norms underscores the importance of recognizing the San Antonio petitioners, Sgt. Green, and Jesse Satterfield's groundbreaking contribution to desegregation in golf in San Antonio, a testament to their resilience and the strides made during a pivotal time in American history.

This epilogue weaves the fictional narrative of Genie and Duane with the real-life legacy of Mr. Jesse Satterfield, honoring his resilience and the significant strides he made in his lifetime. It serves as a testament to the strength and perseverance of those who fought for equality and paved the way for future generations. It stands as the foundation upon which the authors build their lives. As members of the Diaspora, the authors carry forward a legacy of resilience, honor, and the relentless pursuit of equality. Jesse's story is part of America's rich historical tapestry, showcasing the struggles and triumphs of African Americans in the sport of golf.

While Jesse Satterfield may never have won a championship title, his historic contributions to the sport are immeasurable. Jesse played golf until his last days on earth, with his dedication recognized by his employer, Willow Springs Golf Course, where he was valued and trusted throughout his employment. He also worked at Oak Hills Country Club, with which Brackenridge Golf Course is affiliated.

Jesse's love for golf was closely followed by San Antonio news outlets, which even covered his recovery journey from heart issues. Jesse was cherished by his wife, Willie Satterfield, who was a third-generation free-born woman and one of ten grandchildren to Penny Parson, a former enslaved African American known for purchasing significant property in Gonzales, Texas. Although the San Antonio newspaper reported that Jesse "whipped heart trouble," it would later report his passing on January 8, 1957, just three years later.

The news described Jesse as a "clubhouse boy at Willow Springs and Oak Hills Golf Club for many years and promoter of a Negro-pitch-and-putt course," but his family knew him as a devoted son, father, husband, uncle, cousin, and friend. Not a boy. Jesse, a man. He raised four children and supported his wife and community, beloved for his dedication to work and family. His loving wife fainted when the doctor shared the news of her husband's imminent death.

Family members on both sides played golf in Negro tournaments. Jesse's photos were cherished, framed, and passed down to his son Reginald Satterfield, who became known as a provider for his entire family. Reginald, celebrated as a "girl-dad," was deeply rooted in family values and held fast to the teachings and memories passed down through generations. During his memorial, Reginald's daughter described him as a "non-tutu wearing girl dad," remembered by his entire family as "the backbone of his generation and his mother and aunties' generation. A pillar who stood ramrod straight, steeped in his ancestors' convictions, and faithful provider, respected for his integrity, and admired for his commitments." Reginald, like his father, showed love through simple gestures, such as hiring someone to play the Easter Bunny and creating a trail of candy from the front door of his home to his daughters' bedroom.

In summary, the pointed memories of Jesse's son also highlight the enduring spirit, strength, honorable values, and integrity Jesse passed to Reginald, who carried it forward. This is a story that illuminates the legacy of an African American man with reverence for family values, resolute ambition, and rich life lessons. These tools propelled a family, a community, and perhaps even a nation, forward in life.

San Antonio Light (San Antonio, Texas)
1954 > June > 21

Abbott said most refugees from the revolution probably would arrive in New Orleans since the air flight from Guatemala follows that route. However, air service to and from Guatemala has been suspended because of the revolution.

CONSTIPATED?

Robert M. Reed of Gunter, Texas tells how he gets relief

"I'd often get constipated when my everyday schedule was upset—such as by a long trip.

"But I never did get the gentle, speedy relief I wanted until Sal Hepatica was recommended to me.

"Next time I woke up with that logy feeling and knew my day might be ruined by constipation, I took Sal Hepatica before breakfast. Within about an hour, I felt on top of the world! Sal Hepatica does the trick!"

Yes, take sparkling Sal Hepatica before breakfast and feel fine again . . usually within an hour. Or, take it in the evening one-half hour before supper and feel fine by bedtime! Sweetens

---

the fraternity.

12 Negroes Play On S. A. Links

Twelve negro golfers teed off at Willow Springs golf course over the weekend after city council passed a resolution opening municipal golf and tennis courses to negroes.

Willow Springs Employe A. C. Loessberg said 12 negroes, in addition to more than 200 white golfers, made the rounds Sunday. He reported four negroes were playing Monday morning.

Before the council resolution Saturday, it had been the custom to allow negroes to play at Willow on Monday and Tuesday mornings only.

The first two negro golfers teed off from Brackenridge shortly before noon. They were Jesse Satterfield, clubhouse attendant at the Oak Hills Country club, and Sgt. Edward Green, Randolph AFB.

Rabies Perils Vacationing Boy

KANSAS CITY, June 21.—(AP). A Missouri family is on a vacation trip to Florida, unaware that a member is in danger of rabies infection.

All police in southeastern

Negroes Open Fight On Pool Ban

(Continued from Page One)

Bichsel issued the following directive to police:

"Inasmuch as the ordinance is not in effect, no arrests will be made for violation of said ordinance; however, officers will stay in the vicinity of the entrance gate and advise those restricted by ordinance to comply with the ordinance and blockade that gate should such person attempt to enter the pool."

The directive also instructed assigned policemen to notify negroes their money will not be accepted if they try to enter.

FACE ARREST

Police Capt. R. D. Allen said if negroes try to pass the police "blockade" at the pools, arrests could then be made for disturbing the peace.

Outside of negro protests, one of the first denunciations of the segregation ordinance was made by Ben T. Welch, pastor, Cokesbury Methodist church.

In an open letter to the city council, Welch, pointing out he was speaking for himself and not for [...] said:

"As a citizen, I will resist to the last the use of any of

Rebel headquarters claimed government soldiers "are deserting to our side" and declared the Arbenz government had no confidence in its army.

In a statement, the headquarters said the "national liberation movement has taken a position inside the territory of Guatemala without the help or cooperation of any other country or any foreign entity." A spokesman said the rebel force consisted of 5000 men, all Guatemalans.

The Arbenz government has charged Castillo Armas received aid from Nicaragua. It also has asserted the rebel force is composed of adventurers from other Central American nations, in addition to Guatemalan exiles.

AND STAY OUT!

UNITED NATIONS, June 21. (INS)—A blunt warning to Soviet Russia to stay out of the western hemisphere has been issued by U. S. Ambassador Henry Cabot Lodge Jr., in the UN.

Soviet Delegate Semyon K. Tsarapkin was sharply rebuked by Lodge during yesterday's security council debate on Guatemala's charge that Nicaragua and Honduras were guilty of open aggression.

Turning to Tsarapkin Lodge snapped:

"Stay out of this hemisphere and don't try to start your plans and conspiracies over here."

Following the outburst the council passed unanimously a resolution calling for an immediate end to all bloodshed

Jesse Satterfield & female golfer

Negro Golf League

Top row, 4th person from the left: "Uncle Joe" (Joseph Nickson).
Bottom row, 2nd person from the left: Jesse Satterfield Jr. and Jesse Satterfield Sr.

Willie J. Satterfield (Jesse's Wife, Red's mother)
aka "Mother Dear (Madea)

Barbara J. Satterfield & Reginald Satterfield
aka "Red" aka "Reggie" ~ Parents of Rhonda, Monica & DD

Jesse Satterfield's trophies and shoes on front cover

Jesse Satterfield's draft card with redactions for privacy.
Notice: 'Mrs. Willie Satterfield (wife)' and 'Mr. George Hoffman of Willow
Springs Golf Course in San Antonio, Texas'.

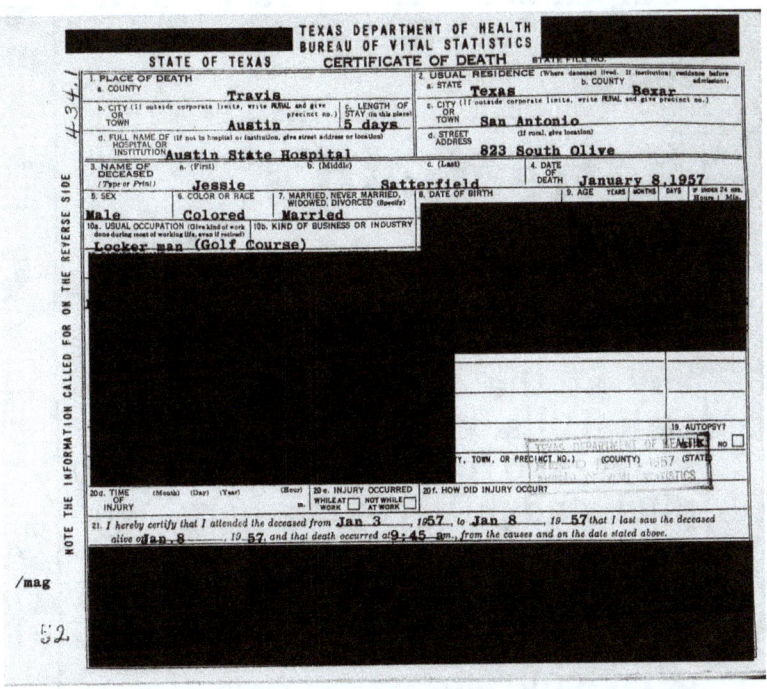

Jesse Satterfield's death certificate with intentional redactions for privacy.
Note misspelling of his first name and job description.

...eapolis and played his
football at the University of
Illinois.

Satterfield's Funeral Monday

Jesse Satterfield, clubhouse boy at the Willow Springs and Oak Hills golf clubs for many years and promoter of a negro pitch-and-putt course here, who died Jan. 8, will be buried Monday, with funeral services at 3:30 p. m. from St. Paul's Methodist church.

All Call For
Family Unity

What is Your Statement For New Millennium

Passing from the 20st century to the 21st, we have observed many changes. For example, do you remember bluing the the wash water, or cooking "faultless" starch , or made margarine with the orange oil color that had to be added? As we approach this new century we chuckle at all life's old daily necessities. We enjoy and relish polyester, and permeate press clothes. We cannot exist without our pagers or cell phones, and not to mention Federal Express that can deliver fresh dinner rolls prepared by Aunt Shirley from Austin Texas to L.A. just in time for Thanksgiving dinner.

As we enter the New Millennium, we stopped to interview others and inquire about their wishes, dreams, resolution and prayers, we also asked each other what we have to be thankful for, here are the replies:

Elmer Avery: I pray that my family and I continue to grow in the ministry which God has place me in.

Rena Avery : Starting this Century I will take life one day at a time. I plan to Be more committed to God. I would like to focus on Christ, as I seek to do more things which will enhance me and my life with others. I plan to do this by balancing my financial, physical, and spiritual life. I would like to see our family closer. Since my brothers and their families have moved further away, I'll probably have to join the electronic era and communicate on the internet, or video conferencing. My scripture: Phil: I can do all things through Christ who strengthen me.

Marie Lewis: (granddaughter of R.A. Nickson, her siblings: Van, Reneta, Ray Jr. Von Charles, and Valerie).."My Millennium wish is for our family to come together without any " glitches"

What are we thankful for? **Barbara Satterfield:** Ecles 3: To everything there is a season and a time. I am thankful for time. God gave me the time to have a beautiful family and many friends. I have had time by the grace of God to grow, and build a marriage that continues to last now 42 years, and to have been blessed with 3 beautiful girls, and 3 grandchildren. I thank God for reuniting me with my sister Joyce my, brother Bernie, and cousin Shirley (in Austin Texas). **Dorothy Stanton:** I am thankful for my family, and I am thankful for God's love, and friendship with the Satterfields. **Mrs. Latrell Gully:** I am thankful to be alive, that I can move around on my own and enjoy daily sunshine. **Reginald Satterfield:** In my 63 years I am thankful for the new Millennuin. I thank God for giving me wisdom, knowledge, my wife Barbara. My life truly began after my marriage and birth of my three beautiful girls. They now have their own lives and life continues. I thank God for their blessings as well. **Otis Harris:** I am grateful to live to see the turn of the Century. (Uncle Otis is 80 something, and provided us with the photo of Pennie Parson, and the historical account. **MotherDear:** I cherish my life, and thankful I can see the new Millennium. My fondest memory is when I was married, and had my children, and when my mother was living (Lonnie Nickson), our life was so beautiful then. I pray that my family is more loving and caring together. **Bill Clark:** "My is fondest memory is when I was about 13 & worked with Jessie Satterfield Sr. on the golf course. We worked in the locker room where Bob Hope and Bing Crosby frequently played. I often look back on those days. Our family was closer then. One of my other fondest memory was when I was an old infantry Sergeant in W.W.II, in the 25th infantry, it was an all-Black infantry. I would like to see our family get back together, talk to each other more".

2

GRATITUDE AND REFLECTION

I would like to extend my deepest gratitude to my parents, Willie James Williams and Eddie Mae Williams, for raising me into the man I am today, especially during the late 1960s, amid the civil rights movement. Their strength and guidance through those years shaped my character and resilience.

A special thank you goes to my wife, Monica Williams, for hanging with me through so many difficult and pleasurable times.

I would also like to honor the memory of two dear friends who have gone on to Glory: Glenn Taylor and Luis Garcia. Though several years have passed since they left us, I still miss them very much.

To my close friends who are still with us—Mike Heath, Tony Farmer, and David Hartnett—thank you for always being there for me through the thick and thin.

Lastly, but certainly not least, I want to acknowledge and give heartfelt thanks to Richard Teams.

— *Duane Williams*

ACKNOWLEDGMENTS

Tee Time Tales

Grandpa Jesse passed away on the same day his first grandson, Louis Wolford, was born. Unfortunately, Jesse Satterfield never had the chance to meet a single one of his grandchildren. As his third grandchild, I am deeply honored to inscribe and publish the first acknowledgment of Grandpa Jesse's invaluable contributions to America, African Americans, and the Civil Rights Movement.

It is thanks to my father—our father—Reginald A. Satterfield, that the legacy of Grandpa Jesse was never allowed to fade. Together with my sisters, Rhonda, DD, and myself, we carry forward this torch. Although daddy—Reginald never had sons to bear the Satterfield name, I proudly continue this legacy in spirit, as my middle name, Regina, carries his.

To my cousins and siblings, whom I intentionally name, I do this so that we each, through blood and lineage, may equally share in this story: Rhonda, myself, DD, Gina, Jesse J, Jesse, and Joi. May the legacy of Grandpa Jesse live on in us all.

My deepest gratitude to Cousin Sherrita Camp, author, historian, educator, and genealogy librarian. Without your passion for family history, my mother, Barbara Satterfield, would not know her family's past, and we as a family wouldn't have the pride we do today. Your research helped unveil the incredible legacy of Julia Snelling and her pursuit of freedom, portions of her legacy now honored in the Smithsonian's National Museum of African American History & Culture. You also pointed me in the right direction to research Grandpa Jesse, for which our family is forever thankful.

A heartfelt thanks to Debbie Countess, Librarian II, Texana/ Genealogy Department, for your invaluable assistance in uncovering the rich history and articles about Grandpa Jesse.

And finally, to my husband and coauthor, Duane: without your unwavering encouragement, support, and dedication, this book wouldn't exist. Through your commitment to my family and your storytelling in *Tee Time Tales*, you've breathed life into our legacy. You have stood by me through the most challenging times, steadfast in your love and support for both our families. For this, and for you, I am eternally grateful.

ABOUT THE AUTHORS

Duane Williams, affectionately called *Mr. Goodbar* is an African American man arguably known most during his youthful years performing as a male exotic dancer and Venice Beach body builder in Southern California. While he retired the stage, Screen Actors Guild, LA fast club scene, and basketball he can still be found enjoying the dance floor with close friends—though not for hire, nor in a spotlight but most definitely practically any day on the greens golfing.

Duane has become known for trading the bachelor life in LA for the love of his life in the Inland Empire. Yet, through it all, his career in real estate investing and mortgage lending has remained a constant, along with the loyal clients and multitude of friends who have stayed by his side over the years.

Duane's *Tee Time Tales* is coauthored and ghostwritten by his wife, Monica—an accomplished author and physician associate. In his adult years Duane was known at Memorial Park gym in Santa Monica for many years playing pick-up basketball on weeknights. Duane transitioned away from basketball after suffering two medical emergencies requiring quick thinking & CPR by his beloved friend and now life-saver Matt Wolf. The remarkable incident, which curiously repeated itself in a Deja vu-like sequence, attracted local news coverage and can be viewed in the documentary section of Monica's *YouTube* channel: https://youtu.be/MapXAV0fI7U?si=9R5BkGTEzBAoi6CH. Once Duane started playing golf, Mr. Reginald Satterfield—Monica's dad, shared stories about his father Jesse Satterfield. Mr. Satterfield encouraged Duane and Monica's family investigate published articles of Jesse Satterfield and thus Duane's Tee Time Tales was created in Mr. Jesse Satterfield's honor.

Monica Guillemin Williams is a dynamic and accomplished professional whose career spans both the medical and legal fields. As a physician associate with experience in obstetrics-gynecology, emergency medicine, neurosurgery, vascular surgery, plastic and reconstructive surgery, Monica brings a wealth of clinical knowledge to her writing. She holds a Bachelor of Science degree in Health Science, completed a specialized surgical residency in trauma surgery, and earned her Juris Doctor degree.

In addition to her medical practice, Monica is has practiced with attorneys in medical malpractice law and intellectual property law. Monica is known for conducting annual workshops in Los Angeles on intellectual property and is entering into estate planning, wills, and trusts. As Monica Payton, she first gained national recognition as a PA in cardiology as a co-author of a research paper published in the *Journal of the American College of Cardiology* and the *Journal of the American Academy of Physician Assistants*. As an avid author & poet under the name Monica Payton, she penned two medical thrillers exploring the ethics of stem cell therapy and cloning, blending her medical expertise with her passion for storytelling.

Beyond her professional achievements, Monica is an adventurist at heart, having completed numerous mountaineering and whitewater rafting expeditions and excelling as an expert skier, not to mention the gorilla trekking, and several African safaris enhancing her creative pursuits. She recently debuted as an amateur photographer with *Safari of a Lifetime*, a captivating children's storybook and companion photography book. *Duane's Tee Time Tales* marks her entry into historical fiction as a ghostwriter, where she combines her unique backgrounds in medicine, law, and history to craft an unforgettable narrative that celebrates resilience and challenges historical narratives.

BIBLIOGRAPHY DUANE'S TEE TIME TALES

Numbered Citations

1. Dean, M. (February 6, 2024) *Timeline of African American Achievements In Golf*, PGA of America. Available at: https://www.pga.com/story/timeline-of-african-american-achievements-in-golf (Accessed: 10/8/2024).
2. Kilgannon, C. (Oct. 31, 2021, updated Nov. 1, 2021) *125 Years After the First College Golf Match, A Rematch*, The New York Times. Available at: https://www.nytimes.com/2021/10/31/sports/golf/yale-columbia-ivy-league.html (Accessed: 10/08/2024).
3. *History - Brown v. Board of Education Re-enactment* (no date) *United States Courts*. Available at: https://www.uscourts.gov/educational-resources/educational-activities/history-brown-v-board-education-re-enactment (Accessed: Accessed 10/8/2024).
4. *Evans, F.* (March 30, 2022, updated June 20, 2023) *Who invented golf?* (2022) *History.com*. Available at: https://www.history.com/news/who-invented-golf-origins. (Accessed 10/8/2024).
5. *PGA Approves Participation of Black Golfers | January 19, 1952* (no date) *History.com*. Available at: https://www.history.com/this-day-in-history/pga-black-golfers-sports-barriers (Accessed 10/8/2024).
6. Williams, L.J. (December 1951) *The Negro in Golf*, The Negro History Bulletin, Association for the Study of African

American Life and History, Vol. 15, No. 3, pp. 52-54. https://www.jstor.org/stable/44212512 (Accessed 10/8/24)

7. Notification of receipt of Petition San Antonio, Petition of San Antonio Negro Golfer's Association

8. San Antonio Light Newspaper

9. *Holmes v. Atlanta Segregation Case is Ruled (7AD)* (1992) *African American Registry*, New York Garland Publishing, An Encyclopedia Historic U.S. Cases 1690-1993 ISBN 0-8240-4430-4, Available at: https://aaregistry.org/story/segregation-on-the-golf-course-holmes-v-atlanta-ruled/ (Accessed 10/8/24).

10. *Holmes v. Atlanta Segregation Case Is Ruled* (1955) *African American Registry*. Available at: https://aaregistry.org/story/segregation-on-the-golf-course-holmes-v-atlanta-ruled/ (Accessed: 03 December 2024).

11. Liebeskind, & K, Kruse, K (1955), (2005) *Holmes v Atlanta Changing the Game*, Modern Portfolio Pro, New York Times, Journal of Urban History

12. Moreno, E. & Warren, C. (September 2016) *Brackenridge Park Golf Course Turns 100, 18 Holes of History*. Available at: https://www.sanantoniomag.com/brackenridge-park-golf-course-turns-100/

13. *Breaking Barriers, a Story in Three Parts* (1949) *Contextualization & Commemoration Initiative*. Available at: https://utincontext.la.utexas.edu/our-work/sweatt-v-painter-gallery-and-entry/sweatt-v-painter-gallery-and-entry/ (Accessed: 03 December 2024).

14. Foundation, T.C.L. (no date) Lions Municipal Golf Course, Lions Municipal Golf Course: *Grounds for Democracy:*

Landslide 2018 (TCLF). Available at: https://www.tclf.org/
sites/default/files/microsites/landslide2018/lions-golf-course.
html (Accessed: 03 December 2024).

15. San Antonio Resolution(s)
    a. June 17, 1954,
    b. Resolution June 19 pages 1 &
    c. Resolution June 19 page 2.

16. San Antonio Light (Tuesday June 22, 1954), page 7

17. Andrews, U.J. (2014) *San Antonio Register (San Antonio, Tex.)*,
    *vol. 24, no. 13, ed. 1 Friday, May 7, 1954, The Portal to Texas
    History*. Vol. 24, No. 20, Ed. 1 Friday, June 25, 1954, Available
    at: https://texashistory.unt.edu/ark:/67531/metapth403786/
    (Accessed: 03 December 2024).

18. *About the exhibit* (1955) *Holmes v Atlanta Changing the Game*.
    Available at: https://sites.gatech.edu/holmesvatlanta/about-
    the-case (Accessed: 03 December 2024).

19. The Portal to Texas History (Friday, July 22, 1955), *Virginians
    Reeling*, San Antonio Register (San Antonio, Tex.), Vol. 25,
    No. 24, Ed. 1, page: 1 of 12. (Accessed: June 13, 2024).

20. San Antonio, Tex. (Friday, October 30, 1953), Vol. 23, No.
    40, Ed. 1

21. San Antonio Light June 21, 1954

22. *Texas Digital Newspaper Program* (no date) *The Portal to Texas
    History*. Available at: https://texashistory.unt.edu/explore/
    collections/TDNP/ (Accessed: 03 December 2024).

23. *Brackenridge Park Cultural Landscape Report | San Antonio*.
    Pg 500 & 546

24. Visit San Antonio, https://www.visitsanantonio.com/blog/post/brackenridge-one-of-americas-most-culturally-significant-parks-celebrates-125-years/

Additional Sources

A. Dawkins, MP, Braddock, J H, II and Gilbert, S (Spring-Summer 2018). *African American Golf Clubs in the Early Development of Black Golf.* Citation Metadata
B. The Western Journal of Black Studies (Vol. 42-2, Issue 1).
C. Dean, M, dptstaff (February 13, 2024) *Black Achievements in The Game of Golf,* The Dallas Post Tribune, NNPA Newswire. https://blackpressusa.com/black-achievements-in-the-game-of-golf/ Accessed Nov 12, 2024. The Williams Record, *Run Newspaper of Williams College Since 1887.* https://williamsrecord.com/463051/sports/an-incomplete-history-of-the-first-black-athletes-at-the-college/ (Accessed: 03 December 2024)
D. San Antonio Express (May 26, 1954) San Antonio, Texas, US. Book 2 of 2. https://newspaperarchive.com/san-antonio-express-may-26-1954-p-1/ (Accessed: June 13, 2024).
E. City Council Ordinance Book (March 15, 1956 - March 29, 1956)
F. National Museum of African American History & Culture published: https://nmaahc.si.edu/explore/stories/leveling-playing-field-golf (Accessed: June 13, 2024).
G. Galveston Daily News, January 20, 1952, Pg. 13, Galveston, Texas.
H. Brown v. Board of Education Supreme Court ruling.

I. San Antonio Light, July 09, 1948, Pg. 11A, San Antonio, Texas.
J. San Antonio Light, July 7, 1953, Pg. 15, San Antonio, Texas.
K. San Antonio Light, Tuesday, June 22, 1954, San Antonio, Texas.
L. Southwestern Bell advertisements, circa 1950s.

COPYRIGHT PERMISSIONS

1. San Antonio Light Newspaper[8]
2. San Antonio Light, Tuesday June 22, 1954, page 7.[16]
3. San Antonio Register, Vol 24 Number 20 Friday June 25, 1954[17]
4. San Antonio, Tex.), Vol. 23, No. 40, Ed. 1 Friday, October 30, 1953[20]
5. San Antonio Light June 21[21]

Additional research gathered
1. San Antonio Light, July 09, 1948, Pg. 11, San Antonio, Texas.
2. San Antonio Light, July 7, 1953, Pg. 15, San Antonio, Texas.
3. San Antonio Light, Tuesday, June 22, 1954, San Antonio, Texas.

The following documents were obtained from Texana Genealogy Department Central Library. Because the documents are a matter of public record they fall outside copyright protection. While the individual documents remain a matter of public record, the specific arrangement, selection, and compilation presented herein are the intellectual property of Vision Harmony. Any reproduction, distribution, or use of this compilation in its arranged form requires prior written permission from this book's copyright owner, Vision Harmony.

Notification of receipt of Petition San Antonio, Petition of San Antonio Negro Golfer's Association[7]

San Antonio Resolution(s)[15]
   a. June 17, 1954
   b. Resolution June 19 pages 1 &
   c. Resolution June 19 page 2.

Jesse Satterfield's Military Draft card published herein was redacted to maintain privacy of the deceased and the family. Because the redaction and placement in this book is specific and unique, Vision Harmony claims copyright protection. No reproduction may be done without consent. However, Military Draft Cards are records which are public information available to anyone upon written request. The Selective Service System publishes on the official website request may be mailed to the National Archives & Records Administration National Archives – Saint Louis. The complete mailing address is located at https://www.sss.gov/history-and-records/

While death certificates are public records and part of vital records Vision Harmony stakes a claim of ownership to the death certificate of Jesse Satterfield as it appears in this book. No reproduction or publication may be made without consent.

The following photographs are the personal property and family heirlooms belonging to the descendants of Jesse and Willie Satterfield. No other persons have legal right or permission to copy, reprint, reproduce or republish without a member of the family's permission.

CREDITS

Editing by Isoke Cullins, M.S.,
www.byisoke.com

Photo manipulation by WAbdullah Aasim @abdullahaasim8,
Instagram@thefantasypulse
Instagram@auraofraven

Cover Design and Interior Layout by Stefany A. Salazar R.
stefanysalazarr.com